VANISHING POINT

JORGE SÁ EARP

Winner of the 6th Nestle Prize for Brazilian Literature

digital ISBN: 978-1-625-17665-3
print ISBN: 978-1-625-17666-0

Original work, *Ponto de Fuga*
© Jorge Sá Earp, 1995
Published by Editora Paz e Terra, S. A.
São Paulo, SP, Brazil

English Translation from Portuguese
© John Jensen, 2014

Bahia Books & Publishing

Translator's Foreword

Brazil's futuristic new capital, Brasilia, was inaugurated in 1960 after four amazing years of construction on a barren plain in the geographical center of the huge country. Little more than a collection of ministry buildings, government apartment houses, and the presidential palace, Brasilia served as the official seat of government. But in reality, it was also a monument to the politician who had it built, President Juscelino Kubitschek, and to the Brazilian people who had dreamed of such a capital for more than 100 years. Nonetheless, it was also a huge finger pointing to the future, a future that in the twenty-first century, more than fifty years later, is already upon us.

Vanishing Point is set in Brasilia in its second decade. By that time, it had taken on the accoutrements of an urban center: malls, shopping centers, restaurants, bars, nightclubs, athletic clubs, universities, and even some of the underbelly of any city—prostitution, hustling, and criminality. Well-heeled politicians continued doing what they had always done—flying in to Brasilia for business, and then returning to Rio, São Paulo, or a dozen other sophisticated home cities. But the regular folks, the bureaucrats, the professors, the business people, even politicians' family members, were stuck there building a middle-class life in a rather forlorn environment lacking most of what they had left behind in their robust home cities that mostly hug the coastline.

In *Vanishing Point,* we come to know a small group of such society builders, most of whom happen to be gay or lesbian, either in or out of the closet. If social life is difficult for the majority of the population, imagine what it is like for the G and L crowd seeking out partners, finding meeting points, trying to keep secrets in a prejudiced and relatively closed small cosmos. Life is often boring to the point that tedium is almost one of the characters of the story, at least in the beginning of the book before things start rolling along. The characters ever seek diversion, which they find through interminable visits to each other's homes, encounters over meals or drinks, afternoons at the athletic club, visits to saunas and bars, or seeking and hanging out with hustlers and prostitutes. Alcohol flows like water, and cigarettes (and sometimes reefer) are ever present.

But it is not all tedium. In the midst of all this, a number of events crucial to the small world we get to know takeplace: muggings, "outings," discovery of secrets, conquests, exchange of partners, suicide attempts, and betrayals. Note that while the narrative is highly sensual and often suggestive, it is hardly erotic and can be read with great enjoyment by any adult of whatever sexual orientation, and will shock no sophisticated reader. Moreover, the book provides a blanket of morality that plays a strong role—a sense of justice and fairness, respect for others, a need for self-control, principles of democracy, and honesty.

The story is told by four main characters who alternate in giving their first-person accounts in each short chapter. Time is basically linear, with some slight overlap, so that the points of view interlace perfectly. However, the reader must discover who the narrator is for each chapter, at times an interesting challenge. We have Renato, the closeted gay married bureaucrat; his long-suffering wife Heloisa[*], who is a professor; Carla, Heloisa's friend, a lesbian, a painter, and the daughter of the shadowy senator; and Julio, a gay professor and friend of the other characters. A number of interesting personalities file through, including Grilo ("Cricket"), a friend of Julio's; Luciano, the music student desired by both Julio and Renato; Inacio, Heloisa's tennis coach; Waldir, the young soldier taken in by Julio; and other less prominent figures.

An important background curtain is the rich culture of Brazil, Latin America's largest and arguably most vibrant land. The author weaves a luxurious texture of references to literature, politics, history, music, and popular culture most well-known to informed Brazilian readers. To aid the foreign reader, notes have been included to explain most of these references. Notes are not provided, however, for universal references not tied to Brazil or Portugal, such as European artists and philosophers. The reader may simply choose to ignore the notes and

---

[*] Most repeatedly used Portuguese names bearing accent marks have been anglicized: Heloísa, Júlio, Mário, Inácio, Brasília, etc.

just enjoy the story, but one who takes the time to look down at the notes will certainly gain more from the book than just the pleasure of the novel, and perhaps will become interested in pursuing other aspects of that exciting Portuguese-speaking country so distinct from its Spanish-speaking neighbors.

CONTENTS

DROUGHT

1

From my room, I see plates of red earth and the bush extending in the distance. The city has two colors: orange-red and grass green. Towering upward are the dead buildings surrounded by their yards of stone and light posts. In just a short time, night will fall on the Quad. Far off, I hear the squeaking of the swings on the playground just now abandoned by the children. I saw the last one run into a building, climb up the stairs, and disappear among the concrete columns. I lay my forehead against the window glass, and I hear a fly buzzing around and hitting stubbornly against it. With my tie loose and my shirt open, I feel so weak that I haven't even bothered to change clothes.

Night falls slowly, spreading its dark blotches among the angles of the Quad. Moths collect around light posts, forming a palpitating ring of confusion. Points of white light appear planted throughout the Quad and along the Northern Axis, which become lost in the darkness and lead to nowhere.

The city is heavy in silence, seemingly suspended in space, sending messages off to the cold stars. It is as if I were floating inside a spaceship gone adrift. Why did I come to inhabit this wasteland, this far-off plain of red earth?

Noise from the kitchen. She has arrived. The woman always moves around freely in that space. She is coming to knock at my door—I'm sure. She's coming to bug me. But I continue to hold my head against the cold glass. Sometimes I half close my eyes and see only the points of white light, the silence of the Quad.

It is a dead city, a city where the population encloses itself in its cement cubicles and goes to sleep. No one goes out to the town. But a car passes and leaves behind a trail of motor noise, another car far off on the Axis.

She moves around in the kitchen. Glasses clatter. Soon she will come to knock at my door and awaken me from this obligatory late-afternoon lethargy. Only in this office am I safe. My refuge. There is nowhere else in the house like this. Here I am all alone, completely alone, with my books and records. (She wanted to set up the hi-fi in the living room and put the records there, but I refused.) From here, I can contemplate calmly the interior of the Quad. The swing on the playground is still squeaking. Could it be that another child has set it in motion again? I didn't notice. I was looking at my deep thoughts that were coming to the surface to meet the night.

I caress my books while waiting for her to interrupt me with her solicitous squawking. It's been a long time since I've read a novel. I've been reading only poetry lately, isolated poems chosen at random. I pick up a volume of Fernando Pessoa[1] and I read:

> *You will always be your own dream.*
> *You live trying to be.*

I lie down on the leather sofa, open the book and put it over my face, and pretend to myself that I am asleep.

She never did knock. She went to the bedroom, closed the door. She moved off into her own silence.

I hear only the light din of the cars on the Axis, and I sense the smell of the rice paper pages. When I was little, my grandmother used to read to me from a book with this same kind of paper, the same aroma. I don't remember the name of the book. It must have been a French novel, because she usually read in French, and everything I know of that language is because of her reading: *J'ai perdu mon livre dans le jardin de ma tante*—no, no, no—*J'ai perdu ma plume dans le jardin de ma tante.*

I sit up on the sofa. The springs creak. I cover my face with my hands. I'm tired. I get a whiskey from the cupboard under the bookshelf. That's where I always keep my bottle of genuine imported scotch. I leave the domestic stuff in the living room for guests. I put

---

[1] Fernando Pessoa (1888–1935): Portuguese poet noted for writing under several different heteronyms with separate styles and topics.

Bach on the record player, and the music jumps off the record and floats like a firefly in the darkness of a forest. I transport myself to the cathedral in Leipzig. I've never been in Leipzig or Dresden, but the music of Johann Sebastian carries me to one of those cities.

She still hasn't knocked. Enclosed in the bedroom, she must be reading or watching television. No, I can't hear the sound from the TV, so she must be reading.

Why has everything ended up in this hollowness, this emptiness, this desert of red sand on the central plain? We hardly ever speak, but I'm not the one who is going to take the initiative. If she wants to separate, let her ask first.

The fly still has not been able to find the open gap in the window, and it keeps beating against the glass.

2

How heavy it is. I travel along these trails between the scrub brush and the red earth. Because of the low sun, I always do my shopping at five in the afternoon. He has already arrived; the light in the office is on. Lately, he's been shutting himself up in there and only coming out to eat and sleep. He has been so quiet in recent months. This paper shopping bag and the cloth tote bag full of Coca-Cola are so heavy. To shorten my way, I always take this path between the scrub brush and the red earth. A mosquito has just bitten my right arm, and I can't move to scratch my skin, so I put the bag and the Coke on the ground and rub the bite. There is a quarter moon hanging in the cobalt blue sky. Is it a quarter growing or diminishing? I never know which it is. Time to cut one's hair, as Jucineia would say. Did Jucineia clean the oven as I told her to? Did she polish the silver and iron the collars of Renato's shirts right? If not, he gets furious with me.

I keep wondering if he still likes me; that is, if he really loves me like before, or at least as he said he loved me or made me believe that he loved me. If he was pretending, he did it very well to the point where I became completely wrapped up in his looks and his hugs and his kisses. Finally, I get in the elevator. It took a lifetime for it to get here, since someone must have not closed the door all the way or even left it wide open for a long time, as I sometimes do myself when I put down three grocery bags from the supermarket to hold it open.

The elevator goes hmmmmm, unlike the one in my old building in Copacabana, where I had always lived. It had metal cables that groaned. The door of this elevator, made of two metal slabs, slides and makes a noise like a spaceship to announce the floor. The door of that old elevator in Copacabana was a dangerous metal grate that gave out a sound like tired gibberish from years of use. For a long time, I was scared of that metal door, which was just as threatening as the blade of a guillotine. My nanny would pull my arm back when I stretched it out to touch the dark, cold metal with my hands. My good nanny Maria, where is she right now while, with great effort, I am opening the elevator with bags of groceries in my arms as I am about to enter my apartment in Brasilia? She had a round face like a peaceful black moon. I liked to tease her, pulling on her round cheeks until she would utter an ouch.

Kitchens are as cold as prisons. I relax in the bathtub. I like the hot water pouring over my body, over my breasts, over my hair, the fluffy towel that wipes my skin, the steamed-up mirror that I wipe off to see my wet face, my straggly hair. In the kitchen, the tiles are so white that they are cold, or so cold that they are white. Here I sit down imprisoned. I pull out the carton of eggs and put it carefully down on the marble counter. I take out the soft plastic bag of milk, the bottle of Coca-Cola, the cans, a bunch of parsley and onions, lettuce, tomatoes, green peppers, packages of rice, beans, and flour. I never liked to cook. Just look at an onion—consider how much quiet threat lies in that root. It reacts when beheaded and cut by the knife with its strong, tear-provoking smell. The root reacts like garlic that has to be peeled and crushed at the bottom of a pan. I hate having my hands smelling of spices, and Renato complains if he finds slices of onion in a dish. He likes home-style food, well-done steaks, beans smashed as for a child, French fries, rice, and eggs fried in butter. I love restaurant food, a plate perfumed with herbs, and sharp-tasting gravies. Renato avoids spending money in restaurants, preferring to spend money on accessories for his car, records, tapes, filters for his camera (his latest fling), clothes, and so on. Sometimes I get away. I get away with Carla to a restaurant on the other side of the lake or even one closer to home. There we have our little outing and drink a lot of wine. We laugh a lot when we are together, and I tell Carla never to get married. Never. We should always have lovers but never marry.

He continues to be locked in his office. I hear classical music— he's just started listening to that now. (Could it be that Renato has brought someone with him into the office? No, he wouldn't do something like that to me...) I lie down on the bed, light a cigarette, and relax. I haven't the least desire to prepare dinner.

Could it be that he won't come out to see me?

3

Just to see him again tonight. Now little points of white light shine on the center of the Quad, surrounded by the wall of buildings against the thick night. The record and the drink finished, I rub my hands and my somewhat dizzy head. I'm still afraid that she is going to knock and invite me to dinner, although the silence from the other side continues. It's better that way. What an absurd situation—two people living isolated from each other in their rooms, fearful of the presence of the other! I look at the whiskey bottle and think about serving myself another dose. No. In a little while, if I stay here, she won't hesitate to look for me. If I go out and drink in town, then I can seek him out. It's been about two weeks since I've seen him, since I met with him in the big Axis on that part near the bus station. Who knows about today? If I don't go out, I'll never know if he is there waiting for me with the file box under his arm.

I cross the hall safely. Heloisa is watching television. Today, she didn't even prepare dinner; she must be depressed, and when that happens, she barely gets out of bed. She was always given to having acute crises of depression. She went to a doctor who prescribed pills and more pills. So then she reached a state that I thought was even worse: anesthetized, immobile like a showroom mannequin.

The mercury vapor lights cut through the windshield of my car as I cross the Axis. Outside are the silhouette of the buildings and the constant pall of silence that lies over the city. Brasilia at night is white lighted signs navigating among deserted buildings. Across the serpentine streets and the big Central Axis, one or another car lets off its distant sound. It is as if one were driving constantly on the same superhighway with both origin and destination unknown. And that silence, that silence of a station always isolated in space. There is no one on the streets; no one comes out of their houses. There is pure, dry air and a starry night. And the headlights of the cars that cross each other on this infinite avenue are like the only sign of life within an abandoned city.

The lights of the *Conjunto Nacional,*[2] the shopping center and meeting spot in the capital, light just like any shopping center in the American Midwest. A few pedestrians walk along after coming out of the movie theater or looking at store windows. I go through the two parking lots designed in a U-shape. I pass in front of the shopping center and to that confusing world of ticket windows and bars on the upper part of the bus station. I take the return road, so I can check whether or not he is there today. No, he is not. Shit. Again. He disappeared over the horizon, that inexorably flat horizon of Brasilia. What was his name again (that is, if it was his real name)?

Thin, dark, the file box under his arm, he was skipping class at the university. At a slow speed, I could see that he was good-looking. I had done that before, as Julio is used to doing. But his stories at first shocked me to the point of feeling angry at Julio, considering him vulgar and unnecessarily descriptive. Then he bored me, and then I finally realized that he excited me, both because of the mystery and the danger involved.

I took another U-turn around the Conjunto Nacional. On one of these nights, restless, I left home and went driving at random. I went to the Gate, sat down at the counter, and drank two whiskies. An older woman, accompanied by a guy with the face of an idiot, watched me the whole time. Her face looked like a real mask, and it seemed that at any moment, it would fall, breaking over the counter like a piece of plaster. My hand huggedthe telephone, lingering a bit—I wanted to call Julio. But I didn't. It was late, and I didn't want to make one of those needy calls in the middle of the dawn. I went back to the Axis and drove to the bus station, and I don't know whether I was thinking of Julio's stories or not. Maybe. That's when I saw him with his file box under his arm.

---

[2] Conjunto Nacional: the first shopping mall built in Brasilia, located across from the bus station.

On my second spin past him, he responded to my look again, and I stopped. I was shaking a little bit; he smiled. I offered him a ride; he got in. Then the Axis, the mercury-vapor lights, the silent buildings, the quiet of a long road were cut by our reluctant dialog. I can't remember his name, but the thing happened right there in the car, in my tiny Fiat, at the edge of the lake near the university.

It was good. It was very good, but I don't remember his name.

4

I can't sleep. It's tough, but that's how it is. I saw everything on TV, from the soaps to the last movie, which I remember really liking the first time I saw it a long time ago, but now I think it's insipid. Actually, I didn't really pay much attention. I drank a cup of milk, had a yogurt, and ate a piece of toast with cheese, and that was it. Sometimes I would take my eyes away from the television to look at the venetian blinds, only to see the reflections on the slats of the headlights of cars passing by. On the North Wing, very few cars go by, giving the impression that we are camped out in a desert, as Renato himself says. Not the case from Carla's windows: the South Wing has a lot of activity.

While watching TV, I felt a little pain coming up from my abdomen into my stomach. I have suffered constantly from cramps since I was little. I remember that in school, on the day before the exams, I had constant horrible intestinal pains that ended up in diarrhea. There were days when I had to run to the bathroom and lock myself in for hours. My classmates must have thought that I was doing something naughty—those who only had sex on their minds. However, the cramps didn't always come because of exams. Not rarely, they came about from unknown causes. I would be feeling happy. Everything would be going well. Then, suddenly, pain would overtake me. My mother thought I should see a doctor, but I never did. I would say to myself, *This is nervous pain; I need a tranquilizer,* and then I would go after my grandmother's Valium. Poor thing. Even today, she walks around our house in Botafogo[3] at night without being able to sleep a bit. She reads a lot (in one of her recent letters, she writes that

---

[3] Botafogo: a beach-front neighborhood in Rio de Janeiro's southern area, north of Copacabana. It has a spectacular marina and a view of Sugarloaf.

she has limited herself to rereading her favorite novels), watches TV until the last program is over, sews, and plays solitaire. A single Valium pill no longer has any effect on her. Nor on me either, so I would take two or three, and the pain would get better.sIt made me feel at peace, at peace with myself. There's no other way.

I ended up having to go to the doctor anyway, a general practitioner, a friend of mine. He prescribed steroids, which calmed my nerves and relieved my frequent depression. After we moved to Brasilia, the pain began to visit me more regularly. I think it's the city. I think it's Renato.

The door slammed. I heard when he went out; I heard when he was walking slowly through the hall like an old woman, like my sleepless old grandmother in Botafogo. He went out. Now he has started going out at night without saying anything to me, just as he did during the first months when we got here.

"I'm going to the movies," he would say, without even inviting me to go.

And I was expected not to ask to go along. Once I dared. "I'm going with you. What movie is it?"

"I'm sorry, Helo, but I feel like going alone. I'm going to buy cigarettes," and he must have gone to Taguatinga or even Lusiânia[4] to buy the cigarettes, because he didn't come back for hours.

"I'm going to take a spin. I need to get some air."

"I'm going with you."

"No, I'm going alone. I'm bored. You prefer I stay at home with a long face? I have to go out, Heloisa! And alone!"

I called my mother, and she told me that that's just how it is. A man needs to feel free; the house can't be a cage for him.

Mom doesn't connect to anything anymore. She just thinks about Bob, her new boyfriend. After separating from Dad, she started out looking for big young hunks on the beach. I don't know what she hopes for in a relationship like that—the boys only want her money. My grandmother is scandalized but doesn't say anything; she just

---

[4] Taguatinga and Lusiânia: "satellite cities" of Brasilia. Taguatinga is in the Federal District, 19 kilometers from Brasilia; Lusiânia is 60 kilometers away in the surrounding state of Goiás.

complains about her aches and pains and her incurable insomnia. And Mom brings the boys home to our old house in Botafogo, leaving Grandma quite perturbed.

Dad, for his part, is getting along very well, thank you, constantly smoking his curved pipe, wearing a tight vest, and working at his insurance company while living with Marluce, his secretary. I never imagined that Marluce would be Dad's lover. Wow, when it all blew up, it was a real scandal! Mom acted like a wildcat. She had always played the part of a grand dame, but now she played a scene worthy of the worst Mexican film. She cried, shouted, broke down in tears, and threw in his face a long list of wrongs—all the dirty laundry—and finally scratched him in the face. A huge drama! I never thought that she loved him, or that I loved him, or that I loved Renato as much as now when I am losing him. I am feeling his presence slip through my fingers like some liquid with his nocturnal escapades—to avoid seeing me, to avoid our face-to-face encounter. Why don't I get up the courage to ask him the head-on questions that he so much fears, the reasons for his nightly outings, his constant isolation in his office, his shabby attempts to avoid dialog? A few months back, he decided to play tennis. Renato, who had never liked sports, not even soccer, although his father would always say that the whole family were crazy fans of the Flamengo soccer team. He is learning tennis for the simple purpose of fleeing from me. And I, like an idiot, never complain, and I accept his behavior condescendingly. Saturday, tennis. Sunday, tennis.

"Come, have lunch with me at the club," he invites.

I go and there is always a table full of friends and acquaintances. At night, he leaves me alone. At least we still share the same bed. Sometimes he takes me in his arms and kisses me furiously, as if he wanted to finish that conjugal task quickly. The last time was good. It was sweet. We came to climax together as had not happened for a long time.

"Do you still have sex?" Carla asked me between swallows.

"Sometimes."

"The husband didn't come around, so then…" Jucineia was telling me the other day about some of her neighbors in Ceilândia.[5]

Worst of all is that ever since I met him, he has been a hell of an attraction to me. When I saw him for the first time—it was in 1970—I found him irresistibly attractive, although his body wasn't all that great. Besides, what really interests me in a man is his intellect, his way of carrying on a conversation, more than the physical part. Not Julio. He looks at the mouth, the height, the body, the line of the nose, the color of the eyes and hair. Well, homosexuals are different. (They feel in a different way; I think they have a different view of the world.) But Renato was simply a turn-on for me. It was that jaunty way of his—half laid-back, nonchalant—that captured me. He was intelligent, cultured. He knew all my favorite authors (only the years have shown me that Renato, although a frequent visitor of bookstores, is really just a devoted reader of dust jackets). He went to the movies and the theater as enthusiastically as I did, and he had seen all my favorite films. I thought I had found my Léon, just like Emma Bovary, on that autumn evening in a French province. (By the way, I have the impression that I lent my bound volume, which belonged to my grandfather, to Julio a long time ago, which he has never returned to me. That's funny, a would-be writer who has never read Flaubert…oh, well.)

So what? Léon! Renato turned out to be so without a will, so indifferent to life with the passing of years, that my reaction was to begin to lose interest in him. And it's only at those times when I feel all alone, or when a fear of future loneliness hits me, that I will feel desperate enough to invite him to come to my side of the bed. Why are we so fragile? We are no more than mere shadows of the men seeking the comfort and stability of a house full of kids, furnished in middle-class style, including the obligatory television set as the main picture in the living room. Can it be that every woman is still stuck in this small-minded ideal of a happy home, no matter how intellectual or independent we want to be? On the other hand, don't men also seek this same tribal shelter, with the little woman at their side cooking the

---

[5] Ceilândia: another satellite city, one of the largest, about 24 kilometers from the center of Brasilia.

rations that will line the stomachs of the tired hunters, the same woman who will cuddle them in bed, comforting them after a day of struggles? So why then do they almost always keep a lover, an ineffable concubine, with a hoarse voice on the telephone, preferably younger, thinner, wearing a red satin bodice? Because the other one filled out, her skin got dry because of drinking, and her teeth turned yellow from smoking. Her hands smell of garlic and onion, and she only combs her hair with colored plastic rollers.

One night, I dreamed that I was a prostitute—a beautiful and tempting prostitute reclining on a scarlet or emerald green *récamier*. I don't remember which. I received one man at a time. That day, I received several men, and they gave me gifts of perfumes in crystal bottles, flowers, and costume jewelry. The last ones who came paid me in cash, and the bills looked dirtier and dirtier the more clients visited me. Dirtier but more numerous. Nonetheless, I laughed and took delight in the game. In the dream—it was funny—I knew that all of that would last only a day, and I made love with all of them without getting tired. I told the dream to Carla, who about died laughing.

The picture-less television hisses in front of me. It's two in the morning, and he hasn't come in yet. I am immobile in bed, unable to sleep. The empty glass whitened with the remains of milk, a crumpled napkin on a plate, the ashtray full of cigarette butts, and my alarm clock on my headboard. I must sleep. Tomorrow, I have to be at the university by eight o'clock. There's no way: I'm going to the closet and get the bottle. In the kitchen, I fill a glass with water, and I take a Valium. I open the window of my room, and I contemplate the silence over the Axis, the mercury-vapor lights, and the darkness of the lake in the distance. A car goes by. Who could that sleepless traveler be, who, like my husband, is looking for someone in the middle of the night? My eyelids are heavy. I bid good night to the brightest star, go to bed, and turn out the lights.

5

I was in the library reading the last pages of a novel by Lucio Cardoso[6] when Heloisa came in. It's funny, she doesn't wear glasses, but she carries a pair, as if the frames were constantly threatening to escape, wanting to flee, floating away. Heloisa cuts her hair badly and wears it up in a ponytail like a hairdo done quickly in the morning. When she uses makeup, it looks as if she is dirtying her eyes, and she is not ugly at all. She even has pretty features.

She comes and throws herself down in front of me, holding her jaw in her closed hands with that affectionate look. She spies the cover of my book and twists her nose.

"You really like him, don't you? I think he is so sick..."

I can't tell her about last night when Renato rang the doorbell around midnight and looked drunk with a bad-humored face. He came in and sat down and wanted whiskey. I asked why he was still wearing a suit, and he said he hadn't felt like changing after work.

He then took a few crumpled pages from his pocket and told me that they were poems of his. The latest. He read to me. Look, I was totally not in the mood to hear poetry last night. I detest listening to poems like that under the best of circumstances, especially by beginners.

He read, read, and read some more, until he got tired. There were about four poems. All were of the type in which one lets off steam, and they were too abstract.

"What do you think? Be frank."

---

[6] Lucio Cardoso (1913–1968): a prolific Brazilian novelist, playwright, and poet from Minas Gerais state. He was known as a Catholic, a conservative, and a homosexual writer. His best-known novel is *Crônica da casa assassinada* (*Chronicle of the Murdered House*), 1959.

"They're not bad," I said. But faced with Renato's disappointed expression, I added, "It is just that I think they need a little more polishing, you know?"

Which does not mean anything, but I couldn't say that the poems were simply immature, written by a guy in love with no other resources available to him than paper and pencil, locked in his office at the end of the work day in this bureaucratic city or in his room suffering from insomnia. Renato is just not a writer, that's all. On the other hand, I felt that he wanted to make a revelation to me. He moved around nervously on the sofa, and he played with the ice cubes in his whiskey, his fifth or sixth drink of the night, for sure. Then he got up, put on an Elis Regina[7] record, lit a cigarette, and went to look out at the starry sky.

I didn't know how to continue the conversation. I had to put Lucio Cardoso aside on the bed. I didn't feel like having a drink, but to keep my hands and head busy, I served myself one. Renato turned around and told me that he had been looking for a girl whom he had met one night at the Conjunto Nacional. She was a student—and he emphasized this detail, I don't know why—who carried a file box under her arm. He had never seen her again. She didn't have a telephone for him to call her, but she was going to call him. He was obsessed.

"And what about Helo?"

He revealed to me that he couldn't stand his marriage any longer, things like that. He couldn't stand to see her. He spent his nights locked in his study, and on weekends, he fled to the tennis club. Nonetheless, he didn't have the courage to talk to her about getting a separation.

"She is so passionate, you know?"

I know and I told him that he should start a serious talk with her. That way, if they separated, things would end without mutually bad feelings. Renato buried his face in his hands and remained silent for a long time. Then, with his eyes fixed on mine, he told me that he envied

---

[7] Elis Regina (1945–1982) became a leading popular singer after 1965 with a string of hits and television performances. She is often regarded as one of the best Brazilian vocalists of all times, and her premature death shocked the country.

me, my freedom, my way of life. I felt awkward. I couldn't confess to him the price of this freedom of mine, which results in a deep loneliness and an incessant search for the "other," who perhaps doesn't even exist. No, I wasn't going to talk about it at that time, although I had in my favor the safety of boring Renato, whose powers of attention and memory are minimal.

I trust him just as I trust Helo. But it's not that. It was either cowardice on my part or a certain sense of social decorum that led me to think that my confession would be inappropriate at dawn. With some difficulty, Renato got up and left.

Heloisa is sorry that she suffers from insomnia with a certain regularity. She was the one who introduced me to Renato. When I saw him for the first time, I thought he was a turn-on. That impression he gives of a suntanned little boy dressed up as an executive, his hands in his pockets, his shoulders wide, and his deep, greenish eyes—wow, I went crazy. And he was my friend's husband. The two of us began to be friends, to go out together for a beer. We talked a lot about books, music, and the movies. He was a well-informed guy and was badly in need of company. Sometimes he would call me on a Saturday to invite me for a beer, and we would stay out for hours and hours, until the sun went down, just talking. Heloisa rarely came along. I met her as soon as she started at the university, and then we became close friends. Months later, she invited me to dinner at her house, just the three of us. Heloisa made a cheese and beef soufflé, I remember well. We drank wine and listened to music—the classics of Bossa Nova.[8] I had the impression that Renato, through his cigarette smoke, watched me the whole night. After a while, I stopped feeling sexual attraction for him, or at least I repressed it, and put in my head that we were just friends.

Heloisa calls to invite me to take a walk around the campus. I haven't the least desire to teach class, and neither has she. The air is beginning to become excessively dry, and soon I'm going to have

---

[8] *Bossa Nova* ('new bump') was a style of Brazilian music of the late 1950s and early 1960s, a sort of soft samba, that garnered a huge international following. Its leaders were Luiz Bonfá, João Gilberto, Antônio Carlos (Tom) Jobim, and Vinícius de Morais, among many others. "The Girl from Ipanema" was the best-known international hit of the genre.

problems with my nose, which bleeds like crazy in August. I hate the dry weather, the vegetation that practically turns into a desert. A friend of mine always says that Brasilia has a desert climate: hot and dry during the day; cool at night. The bare trees, the burned grass, whirlwinds of red earth rising in the air.

My friend lights a cigarette and tells me about her relationship with Renato. She finally repeated her version of their conjugal crisis. This situation is bad; you can't do anything, but I think just listening is good. It's no good for the two of you to continue living together in this heavy atmosphere. That's my opinion.

After my class on Baroque art, I leave the university feeling happy, and at home, I find a note from Pedro. He came by here to talk, and he's going to come back at around seven o'clock. He invites me to dinner. In the mail, I find bills and more bills; no letter from a friend. I get a beer from the refrigerator and call Grilo Falante.[9] He is always involved in some complicated affair; he fought with the maid and wants to move to São Paulo, "where one can really live." Then I call Aldo, who, with his usual squeaky voice, told me quickly that he was going to a Venezuelan diplomat's home for dinner. He lives for these kinds of get-togethers. He told me once that his dream was to be an honorary consul of any country, even of some obscure African republic.

I try to read Lucio Cardoso's poems but can't concentrate, and I stop to contemplate the late afternoon. There is already a brick color shining all around as the sun sets: incandescent Brasilia. The orangish disk—which I see from the window of my apartment—emerges with the horizon far off on the plain. There is not a bit of breeze, and the air remains dry. I go to the window to watch the sun's funeral ceremony. Unmoving, I feel like an Egyptian, a Greek, a Persian, or an Aztec paying homage, fulfilling the sacred ritual of the day. And there goes the red disk disappearing and carrying with it another day, the literature classes, Heloisa, Renato, and Heloisa's cigarette threatening to set fire to the grass.

---

[9] *Grilo Falante*, literally, 'talking cricket', but we'll just call him *Grilo* most of the time, as do the characters.

6

Wasn't it on a Wednesday when I saw him for the first and only time? Anxious, enclosed in that office where the sun beats down violently on the window glass, toasting a room where the air-conditioning has broken down. The new secretary types the last memo of the day nervously and quickly. Teixeira looks at the clock; Guedes picks his teeth with a match; and the office boy yawns, egotistically listening to the radio. The beautiful landscape at the end of the day lights up the room with a red glow. I go to the coffee thermos and serve myself, since Jucelino is so interested in the rebroadcast of the game. The coffee is cold, so I leave the little cup on the tray. I loosen my tie and go to the bathroom, where I find Chaves, with those deep circles around his eyes and his dirt-colored skin, spitting while he talks. I look at the schedule on the table—useless papers, senseless words and numbers.

"Are you not feeling well?" asks Claudete, the newly hired secretary.

I answer no, and she keeps on trying to maintain the conversation and hands me the memo. I let her go for the day. I can't stand that curious look of hers behind the thick lenses of her glasses. It's unbearably hot in the office, even at this time when the sun should be getting weaker.

"I'm going," says José Teixeira, picking up his coat from off the back of his chair.

I listen to him like a merchant. I'm the boss, and I don't want to play the tyrant, but neither do I want to set a bad example. I wait until six o'clock. Then I think about his little devil face. He'll be there today, in front of the Conjunto Nacional, for sure. Waiting for me, yearning for me.

At six o'clock, I leave the ministry, after Jucelino, after Guedes. I get my car out of the parking lot. I stop at the signal on the esplanade, and I see the twilight behind the tower. The lights of the Conjunto Nacional are already on, and they are flashing. In the background is the reddish sky. The cars, at rush hour, break free from the signal and continue along the esplanade. White headlights in the opposite direction, in a lesser number, are on their way to the lake. Red taillights leave their trail in the direction of the two wings.[10] I don't turn right toward the North Wing, but rather to the left, making a U-turn in front of the shopping center. A crowd is gathered at the entrance along the walkway, where there is that sort of open Arabian market.

He's not there yet. I drive through the full parking lots. I go slowly, and I feel a certainty growing within me, as if a few hours with that boy represented complete happiness. Lines of darkness mix with the red splotches. The sun engulfs the falling night. The lights of the Conjunto Nacional get brighter.

There he is—with his file box under his arm, standing on the walkway. He moves as if he were anxiously waiting for someone. (Me, maybe?) I slow down; he sees me. (Shit! What's his name?) He bends over, smiles, and I open the door. He gets in and puts the file box down on his lap.

"Hey, Marcelo," he greets me with my fake name. I don't even remember his fake name.

---

[10] Wings: Brasilia is laid out like a huge airplane with its fuselage and two wings.

24

7

An approximate landscape: not a rectangle framing the imprisoned space of columns in the brush, but rather something that suggests more of a prairie, containing urban elements or some affliction that sometimes takes us by surprise. Or even a game of dice or dominoes, or balloons rising from a park—something like Paul Klee.

Shit, we haven't been able to create anything; the world has run out—we are either saturated or hollow. It's only possible to paint that which has already been done before, and one always ends up evoking some classic artist.

What I really wanted to do was make approximations or suggestions, mixing the figurative with the abstract, in total freedom. Combinations of techniques: drawing, nankeen, oil, acrylics, engraving, collage. Another day, I produced some lithographs. At first, I was pleased, but today I can't stand them. It's just as well that I sold them to help with the monthly bills.

I began to draw this morning but couldn't continue. Something was missing. I watered the plants, peeled an apple, and leaned out the window like a little country girl. (Just imagine if I had been named Mary of Grace and had been born in Águas Claras[11] and now looking out on the town square with the sun overhead shining on the bandstand, and, in the background, the white walls of a church?) I see the Quad and the static landscape surrounded by reinforced concrete. Our civilization produced this admirable state of things: we grow and we multiply; we reproduce by the millions; and we can only live on top of each other in these cement caverns.

The apple dissolves between my moist fingers, the knife, and my mouth, while I think about why I came to live in Brasilia. Well, I had to.

---

[11] Águas Claras: a satellite city located near Brasilia in the Federal District.

I went back to drawing, but nothing came out. It didn't work. So then, I try to finish a painting. I do two strokes and that's it.

The morning weaves lively rays of sun to the sound of birds chirping: the morning tapestry.

I talk with Nicolau in the service area of the apartment at the side of the laundry tub. Today, he doesn't feel like talking. No one feels like talking today, not even me. I turn on the radio. I try to break my boredom. Roberto Carlos[12] sings, and I turn it off.

Deep inside, I miss her. So I light a cigarette and look at a painting without focusing on it. Funny, at first he was the one I was attracted to. As I got to know them, I become more and more involved with her, but I don't know how. For a long time, it's true—I haven't felt anything for a woman.

It happened at that book signing for the diplomat who writes poetry. I was totally discouraged, but Julio insisted so hard, saying that the guy was good, that there would be a lot of interesting people there, and that I wasn't doing anything on Wednesday anyway. Evidently, the little book was terrible, but at least Julio introduced me to Renato and Heloisa—the grand find of the evening. We began to talk about vanguard, experimental literature, the *nouveau roman*, until I actually confessed my passion for Marguerite Duras and, especially, for the *Moderato Cantabile*. Everything was the fault of my Frenchified upbringing, for I had lived in Paris and Geneva.

With a glass of whiskey in my hand, and with the ice cubes tinkling, I got close to Renato's face on purpose to tell him about my impressions from reading that novel. Heloisa seemed unappreciative of my easy intimacy.

Julio suggested that we go out to eat, and he went with me in my indefatigable VW Beetle, the couple having gone ahead in their station wagon. We stopped at Fritz's. I couldn't take my eyes off Renato. Heloisa at first looked half idiotic to me with those crooked eyes, empty look, and awkward posture.

---

[12] Roberto Carlos (1941–): undoubtedly the most famous pop singer in Brazil and a Grammy award winner. He burst on the music scene in the mid-1960s as a pop-rock singer and evolved into a balladeer as he and his fans aged. He is also very popular in Spanish-speaking countries.

We talked about the *nouveau roman* and the vanguard. Julio attacked American art, favoring the European. Renato vehemently counterattacked; he likes Pollock and Man Ray. Julio hates them, as he also hates Nathalie Sarraute and Robbe-Grillet. The discussion went on from there. We even talked about preferences between Portugal and Spain—Julio preferring the former, thanks to his loyalty to Camões[13] and Fernando Pessoa, and Renato the latter national literature. Stupid. But Julio ended up putting on a show. Drunk as he was, he admitted that between the welt of a shoe and castanets, he preferred to play castanets with a comb in his hair and a skirt on. And between reading Nathalie Sarraute and Fernando Pessoa, the best thing to do was to listen to Marlene[14] singing "Jura." Heloisa shut up, turned red, and pinched Renato, a sign that it was time to leave, since the guy was getting weird. I was laughing out loud, and so was Renato, which only increased my interest in him. So the intellectual conversation ended up as a tremendous idiocy. I hate serious matters during a night that has every reason to be relaxed. Julio kept on saying dumb things; Heloisa barely avoided hiding under the table. She finally hugged Renato, gathering herself under her husband's wing.

I frankly considered her a stool pigeon. Julio sometimes shocks people who don't know him well. I always tell him that, but it doesn't do any good. But then, why would it?

If she doesn't call me, I won't call her. Lunacy. She hasn't called me for a long time.

Heloisa needed someone to type a paper for her master's at the university—Julio had told me so. I offered to do it—I need money as usual. In slack hours at the office, I typed her paper, written in a handwriting that was hard to understand. Reflections on the Discourse of the Historian, right and left postures, characteristic jargon, et cetera,

---

[13] Luís Vaz de Camões (1524–1580): considered the greatest poet in the Portuguese language. He wrote the national epic *Os Lusíadas (The Lusiads),* 1572, a book-length poem that sings praises of the exploits of the Portuguese explorer Vasco da Gama and of Portuguese navigation in general. He also wrote love poems and others.

[14] Marlene (Victoria Delfino dos Santos) (1924–): a prolific Brazilian singer and recording artist. She was especially prominent during the heyday of radio.

et cetera. An enormous bore. As I typed, I thought about how someone could waste so much time and effort for this stuff. An immense bibliography, detailed. I mentioned my opinion to Heloisa one Saturday afternoon at her house.

"You have a lovely view of the lake."

"But only from here in the living room. From the bedroom, we only see the Quad, which is terrible. And this Northern Wing is a desert…"

She offered me coffee or a Coke. I thanked her and answered that I didn't want either.

"Do you have whiskey?"

Heloisa expresses doubts about the focus of her interest in history. She herself considered the paper that I was typing to be boring, done simply out of obligation. Her thesis would be about secret societies at the time of the empire, primarily during the First Reign,[15] much more interesting than those studies that only cover language, discourse, mass movements, and economic and social causes. Then we talked about women in our history, the Marquise of Santos, D. Carlota Joaquina, Princess Isabel, Anita Garibaldi, Maria Quitéria.[16] We discussed such futile things as the physical appearance of D. Leopoldina, evidently at a disadvantage compared to D. Amélia.

Then we turned to domestic topics—decorating plants. We leaned out the window. Heloisa suggested we take a ride around the lake, at that time a cobalt blue in color. During the ride, she confessed that Renato didn't keep her company, which sounded like the usual complaints of a housewife.

We stayed in contact because of the paper. Heloisa showed a sense of humor. A certain affinity developed between us. She came to visit me on weekends and gave me some hints about my house (I'm a terrible manager). She told funny stories about her students, and she talked with

---

[15] Empire, first reign: after independence from Portugal in 1822 until the founding of the republic in 1889, Brazil was governed by emperors descended from the royal family of Portugal. The empire was divided into two reigns: the first under D. Pedro I; the second under D. Pedro II, his son.

[16] Marquise…Quitéria: women famous in Brazilian history, either members of the ruling pre-republic royal family, or their consorts.

Nicolau. In the meantime, I remember that what immediately struck me was her taste in music. Heloisa adored John Lennon, like me, and Cat Stevens, Caetano Veloso, and Gilberto Gil.[17] We remembered old songs, traded records, and recorded tapes for each other. In a word, we became friends.

Even though there was no more real need for me to type her papers, Heloisa continued asking me to do some of her work, just so we wouldn't lose contact, which I did gladly. We called each other almost every day. I really began to like her. Renato seemed to me— and the comparison was inevitable—somewhat superficial and vain, while Heloisa showed real substance.

For a time, I would often go to eat at their home. They must not have thought of me as an intruder, since they sometimes even invited me. Yes, I fear seeming to be out of place, as a single woman. One night—and this was funny—Renato invited a French couple over for dinner. He was an employee of some international agency, I don't know which. The couple, of course, arrived punctually at the appointed time, but I, of course, got there forty-five minutes later.[18] While waiting for me, Renato decided to talk about me—he said that I was a painter, and that I also worked for the government, et cetera, but that I sometimes liked to drink a little. It so happened that the Brazilian all-star soccer team had won that afternoon. We watched the game in the office, and then, after the victory, we went out to celebrate. Well, of course, I drank a little too much, and I showed up at Renato's house really beyond the pale. I got sick in the elevator (I had mixed *caipirinha*[19] with domestic whiskey, shit), and they took a long time to answer their doorbell. I felt my vomit rising and rising, until, when

---

[17] Caetano Veloso (1942–) and Gilberto Gil (1942–): famous politicized male singers, musicians, and composers of the *Tropicalia* movement of the late 1960s and 1970s. Both were jailed and exiled by the harsh military regime (1964–1984) and are still performing in Brazil and internationally. Gil was named minister of culture under President Lula in 2003.

[18] It is legendary in Brazil that foreigners tend to show up at the appointed time for social events, while Brazilians are notoriously—and fashionably—late. Foreigners may well find their hosts totally unprepared for their on-time arrival.

[19] *Caipirinha*: a popular Brazilian mixed drink made from *cachaça* (rum), sugar, and lemon juice.

Renato finally opened the door, I flew inside the living room and barely had time to throw up in a planter—as I had done once before on another night. According to Renato, the ferns grew like crazy.

The French couple became unwound and did not know how to react to that barbaric scene. The so-called friend breaks into the living room, completely inebriated, throws herself over the planter, and dumps her insides out, fainting lifelessly. This was my calling card. I put "Imagine" on the record player, sit down on the sofa, and light another cigarette. I look at the smoke and the clean sky through the window. I cross my legs, put my foot on my opposite knee, and think about inviting Julio to lunch, since my pride doesn't allow me to pick up the phone and dial Heloisa number again.

8

The day awakens with an uncomfortable light. He has already left for the club. The venetian blind, blown by the breeze, hits monotonously against the wall. I pass my hand over the empty side of the bed, and I feel the rumpled sheets. He sleeps restlessly. I try to sleep but end up simply crumpling the sheets up even more.

No, I'm not going to the club to chase after him. I'm going to stay home, as if I were not bothered by his absence. The blinds in the living room are also beating annoyingly.

I pick up the book about the Middle Ages that I am reading and get a little distracted by it. Then I go to the window and look out at the lake. Lunchtime is a social occasion, a good excuse to seek others' company. No, I have to learn to live alone. I've been reading this book for centuries, and I'll never finish it.

I make coffee. The telephone sits on the bookcase in the hall. Should I call Carla and Julio to invite them to eat out, since my husband has abandoned me to go play tennis with his friends? Because he prefers the company of those jocks at the club and those futile woman over mine? In Rio, we lived together so well. On Saturday, if we didn't go to the beach, we would take a stroll through Ipanema, stopping at the bookstores and the shops, and we ate lunch either there or in Leblon.[20] Or else we went up to the Alto da Boa Vista or to the Botanical Garden,[21] where we had memories of childhood. Those are things I like better than going to the beach. The hot sun, the sand, and

---

[20] Ipanema and Leblon: neighboring beaches in Rio de Janeiro just south of Copacabana, featuring luxury apartments and boutiques, as well as lovely, white-sand beaches.

[21] Alto da Boa Vista and Botanical Garden: spots to relax in Rio de Janeiro. The Alto da Boa Vista is a park in Tijuca Forest overlooking the city; the Botanical Garden is a beautiful refuge in the southern part of the city.

the cold water bother me. Besides, you come home all sticky from oil and salt, if your skin is not burning. I'm also afraid of the heavy surf. I don't know how to swim; the big waves scare me. And when I was small, I was carried once into a channel full of heavy currents. With great effort, a lifeguard was able to pull me out. As I recall, he was very good looking. Too bad the same one doesn't reappear right now, or another similar one.

One night, we had dinner at a fancy restaurant—the kind I thought existed only in novels and the society columns. If I'm not mistaken, it was to celebrate the eight years since we started going out. Renato never wanted to get engaged. Also, our courtship went on so long that my grandmother suspected that he was a married man.

"I know his family. They live on Fonte da Saudade."[22]

"That doesn't mean a thing, my girl. How do know but that he has something going in the North Zone?" she asked, blowing smoke from a silver cigarette holder and showing her disagreeable smallness.

I put down the book on the Middle Ages; I live so much with history all week. So then I pick up the novel by Lucio Cardoso that Julio lent me. Should I call Carla? She sometimes acts so strange, mostly when she drinks. I don't know. Carla is kind of rude; she overwhelms me a little, and I often feel like never again seeing her. In the meantime, she really listens to me when I open up to talk about my relationship with Renato. Not always the case with Julio. He's always so worried about his little problems, his lightning affairs, that he gets distracted when I begin to talk too much about my marriage, about my specific little whirlwind.

I get up and put on John Lennon: it's the only way to cover up the noise of the blind at the window.

---

[22] Fonte da Saudade (Fountain of Nostalgia): a famous upscale street in Rio facing the lagoon near Copacabana. It inspired a 1986 film of the same name.

9

Whenever I hear that piece of music, I freeze all movement and remain at an absolute state of attention. It normally gets me up in the morning to go to my window, and it tickles my ears like a feather floating on a breeze. I imagine that it is being played just for me. Sometimes I hear it at night, and I pretend that the sounds combine for the single purpose of rocking me to sleep. I know, on the other hand, that he is far from thinking of me when he plucks the strings of his guitar. He doesn't even notice my presence if we should meet at the elevator, the building entrance, or the garage. He always walks with his head down, a furtive look, and that constant little cough.

I saw him for the first time at the university, taking exams, although he was not my student. I needed to give a message to the drafting professor, and I noticed him in the study hall, bent over his paper, holding hard on to his pen, his face tense. I am a terrible reader of faces, and, although I often forget names, people's features never leave my memory. So the day I happened to run into him at the building entrance, I recognized him immediately and discovered that he lives in the apartment directly below mine, which he shares with two friends. The others are noisier; they listen to rock and smoke all afternoon on Saturdays and Sundays. And they don't look at all like him.

One time, I found a letter left in my box by mistake. Full of hope, I imagined that it was for him. I went running down the stairs, but it wasn't for him; it was for his roommate. What could his name be?

I told Grilo about my neighbor and said that I was not exactly falling in love with him, since we had never even exchanged words, but I was getting interested in him. Grilo says:

"Eso es un sueño que hay que ser olvidado." Grilo sometimes likes to speak Spanish.

The problem is that I am beginning to be obsessed. I broke up with Lauro about a week ago, because our relationship was going sour. A huge mistake. I just didn't like Lauro—that was it. The night I met him, I was drunk, and I think I stayed drunk all through our affair. But I don't know how I was able to put up with him for three weeks. He suffers from chronic Marxism, with all the symptoms and stereotypes of the doctrine. I couldn't take it.

"All of your problems are typical of the *petite bourgeoisie*," he would say. "Your poetry goes no further than the problems of the *petite bourgeoisie*."

Boring little guy. And he even badmouthed me to Heloisa. No less than Heloisa, who obviously told me everything, asking why I had been so hard on poor Lauro.

I met him at a night club, after a dinner with my aunt who was passing through Brasilia. There he was, under the flashing lights, thin, pale, wearing glasses. I invited him to my apartment a few hours later. The next day, however, was Carla's birthday party at her father's place in the country. She was going crazy when I got there quite late with Renatinho and Helo.

"Do you think I'm making a mistake by breaking up with Lauro? Tell me frankly."

"I think that you should give it some more time," advised Heloisa.

I took a shit. I'm not giving it any more time. I made a date with him at the vegetarian restaurant that he likes on the top floor of a tall building in the center. There was a poster with deer on it behind Lauro. I mumbled some words and finally pronounced the end of our relationship.

He stopped playing. I run to the window—a stupid reaction—as if I could see him, but I only have the Quad to look out on in front of me, the relentless Quad, with its geometric monotony. The musician interrupted his Bach to take a piss or to drink a glass of water. Suddenly, as I was straightening a picture in the living room, I spy his figure on the grass in front of the building. Isn't that him? It is. He's walking the dog, a brown cocker spaniel. How can he keep a dog while living with two roommates? I ask. I lean out the window and look at him. His back is to me. Clouds that look like ears, rats, and a rabbit blow through a clear sky. The grass, however, looks more and more yellow. The branches of the trees are more twisted from the drought. The pungent air invades my nose. In a few days, it will start to bleed for sure.

The telephone and the doorbell ring at the same time. I can still see him moving across the rectangles of grass for the last time, and now is crossing the cement crosswalk, followed by the cocker spaniel.

It's Hildo at the door, my colleague from the university.

"Wait a second. The phone is ringing."

It's Carla inviting me to lunch. I ask Hildo if he wants to go with us. Already sitting down in the living room, he hesitates. I know he has a certain problem with Carla, but he decides to accept the invitation, as if to say, "What the heck?"

Hildo carries a newspaper under his arm. Today, it brings the news that the government is about to fall, and that Azevedo is quitting. Hildo almost shouts and makes bombastic declarations. At the same time that he is sharing his political opinion, he criticizes the layout of my pictures on the wall or an old dirt spot on the sofa.

"That stain is still there from the party six months ago, huh, Julio?"

"What do I know, dude? Must be. The maid tried to remove it but couldn't."

"Do you still have that poor girl from the state of Piauí? That woman is the doorway to hell, Julio! She's a pig from wherever. The other day, I saw her downstairs talking with Diamantino and picking snot out of her nose!"

"Would you like something to drink?"

"No, I'm not drinking. Thanks anyway." He opened up the newspapers on the floor and bent down to read them.

"Well, I'm going to have a vodka while I wait for Carla."

"Look down there—it's Luciano walking the dog. It's a good thing he's taking that mongrel out for a walk! That dog shits all over the stairwell and the hall. It's disgusting! Their apartment smells like piss, have you noticed?"

Hildo's voice echoed through the hallway into the kitchen where I was preparing my vodka.

"Do you know the boy?"

"Luciano Borges, second year architecture. He's also studying musical theory with Baranowski, and he plays classical guitar. He shares his apartment with two other guys: one studying history and the other with him in architecture."

"How do you know all that?"

"His roommate is my student."

I stopped in the middle of the living room with the sweaty glass in my hand. I didn't want to have discovered his name in such a prosaic way—through Hildo's booming voice. Luciano Borges. I wanted to go to the window again, but I held back. It was enough to have the weapon that I had available starting today: his name.

Carla honked downstairs. Hildo folded his newspapers, and we went down in the elevator. Every morning, Hildo buys four newspapers. He says he reads them all.

We sat down in the patio at Fritz's place. I ordered an ice-cold beer to cool off from the heat and the dry air. Carla asked for a *caipirinha,* and Hildo stuck stoically with his *guaraná*[23] soft drink. The waiter brought the usual little salmon and tuna pies, black and green olives, and slices of black bread. Hildo complains about the sameness of the menu, and he can't decide on anything. I hope they stop this mutual stubbornness and clear the air; otherwise, the lunch is going to be a bitch.

I try to raise everyone up into topics that everyone likes. Hildo then talks about Italian neorealism. Carla talks about French cinema. An exchange of fire. Hildo breaks down and his stoicism weakens, and he finally gives in: he raises his finger to the waiter and orders a beer.

Our Mephistopheles here exhibits an enigmatic smile while pulling on his mustache (figuratively, of course). The conversation continues on cinema. Hildo asks for an *Eisbein* and Carla a *Leberkäse*, and I ask for *wiener Schnietzel* with sauerkraut and potatoes.

Their hunger, in the meantime, must have ignited their political ardor: Hildo defends the Trotsky line; Carla aligns herself with the French socialists—she has Sartre and Camus on her nightstand. Hildo is an avid devourer of Communist compendia, and Carla had an affair

---

[23] *Guaraná*: a fruit that grows in the Amazon. Guaraná extract is considered a health supplement and is used to flavor the national soft drink of the same name, available in a number of different brands.

with one of the participants in the Movement of 1968. Hildo, with his eloquent Bahian[24] blood, does not deny the glory of Rui Barbosa,[25] and goes on in high-sounding discourse. He has verve; he raises his round face, fixes his glasses while wrinkling his nose, and brings his fingers together like an Italian. He dreams of a career in politics.

"I would never vote for you," I say. "Such an extremist!"

He laughs out loud and touches his glass to mine. There is a warm mist hanging over the lake. The vegetation on the empty land in front of us looks almost toasted.

I come back from lunch dizzy; we had drunk a cognac for our digestion. I faint on the bed, but not before building a scene in the novel that I am writing and grumbling. Crap! I didn't want to discover the name of that guy from Hildo's mouth. I didn't want to find it out in such a nontheatrical way.

---

[24] Bahian: from the state of Bahia in Northeast Brazil. Since the state was the original seat of government under the Portuguese and the center of black slavery, it reflects a strong colonial and African cultural heritage.

[25] Rui Barbosa (1849–1923): Bahian writer and statesman, and ardent defender of human rights. He worked for the abolition of slavery in Brazil (which occurred in 1888).

10

Night came on, and I didn't notice: I was reading Cecília Meireles,[26] whom she likes so much. I got distracted and didn't see night fall, and the city come to its own defense with its lights. I hadn't slept after my lunch with Heloisa. She told me she wanted to take a nap. I don't know how people manage to sleep during the day, like Julio. That anthology of Cecília's just sent me into other spheres, and not that of Morpheus.

I invited them to my country place tomorrow for a barbecue. Renato and Heloisa were to confirm with me, and Julio and Hildo will certainly be there.

I think it's so strange how she throws herself at me, the way she sends intense looks my way. Today, I told her how pretty her eyes are without glasses. Women can say things like that to each other. Heloisa smiled and, of course, took off her glasses.

"I've tried to use contact lenses, but they don't work for me. Not even soft contacts."

"That's too bad. You should try again. These days they have some…" I suggested.

We went out to eat beef jerky with beans. We looked for a table at the *Churrascaria do Lago* but couldn't find one: impossible on Saturday at four in the afternoon. I love that bottled butter that people pour over their meat, and that fine *farofa* called *paçoca.*[27] We drank beer, seeking relief from the heat. Flies buzzed between us in the dry

---

[26] Cecília Meireles (1901–1964): considered the best woman poet of Brazil, and one of the best in the Portuguese language. She was a member of the Modernist movement.

[27] *Farofa* and *paçoca: farofa* is a dry side dish made of cassava flour, fried with butter, onions, and other condiments, and usually served on beans; *paçoca* is a version of *farofa* that includes sun-dried beef in the mix.

air. The waiter from Paraíba[28] was looking at the clock and yawning, leaning against the wall at the back. Heloisa does not put her glasses back on and challenges me with her black gazelle-like eyes. I don't know what else I can do. Her hand was placed randomly on the butter-stained tablecloth. Should I grab her and cover her with wet kisses? No. I hold back, thinking of our friendship, all the social mores that keep me from completing the gesture. It could be decisive. Besides that, there is Renato, her husband. I fall in love with a married woman; only I would do something like that.

After all, just what the hell do I see in Heloisa?

Could it be precisely the complexity of the situation that challenges me and leads me to delve fearlessly into those dark waters? I'm going to suffer, of course. A few months from now, the passion will ease, saturated in itself, small unsatisfied pleasures, and it will slide outwards without limits, reaching not its intended target, but other surrounding objects. I'll set the house on fire, that's what.

Heloisa knows how to listen better than anyone. She patiently sets her black eyes on me, and, without taking her attention elsewhere, she picks up on my hollow words, my useless day-to-day and family problems, not forgetting a single detail. The other day, she repeated the names of all my brothers and sisters and all the details of a stupid argument I had with one of them, Ricardo.

I know that she misses nothing. Heloisa is tied to the rest of the world with a blind knot. But she never lets go of her alliances.

I call a friend, but she doesn't answer. I get in my car and drive toward the Axis without any destination in mind. I think about going to a movie or visiting a bar. The mercury-vapor lights shine through the windshield, the road is lost in darkness, and the radio plays an old song. Tired of driving from the Southern Wing to the Northern Wing, I park in front of the Brasilia Cine, where they are showing *The American Friend* by that new German director Wim Wenders.

---

[28] Paraíba: a poor northeastern state with a lot of out-migration to more prosperous areas. Such migrants often encounter discrimination at their destination due to their stigmatized appearance, manner, and accent. The word *Paraíba* is sometimes used as a generic (and pejorative) term for any migrant from the Northeast.

11

I've been thinking only of him in recent days. I can't get away from that obsessive desire. Consequently, that aversion to my wife increases. When she cuddles up to me, picking up my arm, and laying her head on my shoulder to watch television, my first impulse is to move away from her to avoid contact. However, she seems not to notice or pretends to ignore my growing negative feelings.

She walks through the room naked, as if to provoke me. The morning is radiantly blue, and the blinds bang against the wall, blown by a breeze off the lake. That monotonous noise echoes throughout the apartment, reminding me of the weight of tedium of this city, and leading me quickly to turn on the record player.

We made love on Friday. She came on to me. Quick and easy. Afterwards, I turned my back to her, but she drooled down my neck. I pushed her away, and we went to sleep. Yesterday, I spent the whole day at the club. I played a double with Carlinhos in the morning. He won. We went to drink beer with the gang at the side of the pool. Because Heloisa had not come by, although she usually comes in around beer time, we formed a big table and had lunch. I like Selma, Carlinhos's wife; she is very funny.

But I think only about him, even at times when I am with friends at the club or any other place. I only think about Marcelo, and the last night we spent together in that motel. It's funny that his name is Marcelo, precisely the false name that I pull out of my pocket for these nocturnal excursions. He laughed at my lie. I told him everything on our second encounter. He didn't seem to care that I am married. He looked at me with his shy-little-boy eyes. He told me about his family, about his three brothers. His father is a military man, but, unlike his mother, he doesn't know about Marcelo. Of his brothers, no one else is like him. At least, so far, no one has come out.

"That's what you think," I teased.

"No, they're not. They have girlfriends and like soccer."

"I like soccer, too."

Marcelo likes dumb American music. When I asked him if he was familiar with Mozart or Beethoven, he twisted his nose.

"We can't listen to music together," I said.

To tell the truth, Julio was the one who introduced me to classical music.

My grandfather had some records, but mostly of lighter music—pieces by Strauss, Tchaikovsky, Offenbach, Liszt. I remember that he liked to spend his Sundays with them in that old apartment in Copacabana, listening to that music, which, with my child's sensibility, I thought was music exclusively for ballet. My grandmother would read novels by Paul Bourget to me, or French poetry. She would put her index finger to her lips, asking my grandfather to lower the volume of the music on the old record player.

"But I can't hear the pianissimo that way," he protested.

"But think of the neighbors!" my grandmother replied.

It used to be that I only liked jazz, as I still do today. Heloisa doesn't like any kind of music. Like my grandmother, she always asks to turn the volume down. That's why I set up my sound system in my room, far from her imprecations and nervous gestures. I told Marcelo all of this.

"What a shitty wife you must have."

I kissed him, and he got dressed in the semidarkness.

Heloisa asks me to dress quickly, since we are going to Carla's place in the country. Who said I felt like going? No one asked me…Heloisa insists and grumbles.

We go up to Sobradinho; we take the dirt road and enter the rocky drive shaded by mango trees, which leads to the white and blue one-story colonial house. The sun traced a diagonal stripe on the wall. Carla, wearing a long shirt and yellow Bermuda shorts, is waiting for us in front of the door, squinting because of the brightness. She greets us with her usual excitement, her arms open. We enter through the kitchen to leave the things that Carla had asked us to bring. I love a wood stove on an old ranch. Carla's father made a great discovery: he found this little place with colonial construction abandoned among the tall brush. He chopped down the undergrowth; had grass, ferns, and bougainvilleas planted; and he restored the house.

A subdued, oblique light penetrates the window screen in the kitchen and goes to rest on a basket of *jabuticabas.*[29] The black berries shine. Carla squeezes lemons for the *caipirinha.* The houseman—she tells us—is going to fry sausages on the barbecue.

Carla takes canvas chairs out to the terrace. We then sit down in the sun, looking at the lawn and the huge ancient tree. The sprinkler spins around, watering the yard. The blue sky makes me want to drink beer, and Carla brings me a sweating mug with foam up to the top. Heloisa doesn't drink anything, as usual, only lemon soda. She stretches her arms out along the chair and reclines her head to tan her face.

A bee buzzes in front of me; I scare it off, and it goes to bother a plot of daisies.

Carla puts on her bathing suit and plays under the sprinkler. I go to meet her, turn off the tap, take the sprinkler off the hose, and squirt the water directly on top of Carla, who jumps like a lizard, laughing.

I go put on my suit, and she also gives me a bath. The beer and the water are very refreshing. Heloisa remains seated, giving the impression that she is going through one of her long, unexpected absences. Let her be damned. I ask about Julio and Hildo. Carla answers that they should be coming soon.

I walk around the little ranch. I go around the house and through the part of the yard shaded by trees—*jabuticabas, pitangas,*[30] and mangos—and I get to the shelter where Getulio is frying the sausage. Seen from a distance, his silhouette, long and tall, reminds me of none other than Don Quixote. Not only his silhouette, I decide when I get close, but also his face. He lacks only the fine mustache and the spacey look. The smell of the sausage makes me hungry.

---

[29] *Jabuticaba*: a tropical fruit that grows on a tree; also known as a Grape Tree or Brazilian grape tree. Curiously, the fruit sprouts from the tree trunk.

[30] *Pitanga*: a tropical fruit, small and red, growing on low bushes. It is also known as a Suriname or Brazilian cherry and is often used as a hedge in Florida and other semitropical areas.

In silence, Getulio extends his thin arm to me, holding a shiny, greasy piece of sausage on a skewer. I pick it off with care and chew it with pleasure, before returning to the women, who are stretched out in the sun. I think about refilling my mug with beer, but I realize that Heloisa is watching me with the palm of her hand shading her eyes. I feel like she wants to ask me where I am going even though it is obvious. I pretend not to notice her intentions and continue on to the kitchen.

The working-class Quixote approaches with his slow step, carrying a tray of his famous sausage. Flies land with abandon on our appetizer. Carla is surprised; she jabs a piece of sausage with a stick and eats it gluttonously. Heloisa takes a stretch, as if she had been napping. The sun has gotten hotter and makes me want to get under the sprinkler again. We hear a noise of a car, and then Julio's dented old VW comes haltingly down the rocky drive under the mango trees.

Hildo Leão's voice booms in the distance like the warning of a seaman from the top of the mast. The pair demand beer from the hostess and unceremoniously make themselves comfortable on our sun-drenched terrace. Hildo tries to give an account of the latest political happenings—he who reads four newspapers every morning. Carla shows interest in the possible fall of the minister of finance. Julio and Heloisa get together in a private chat. They always have secrets. As for me, I am quite content with my ice-cold beer and fat roasted sausages. My attention moves from this *apéritif sur l'herbe* to the last night I spent with Marcelo in that motel at kilometer X on the Brasilia-Belo Horizonte highway. I feel infinite affection for the boy, and I don't know what may happen later. I play and hope to win. And if his parents one day discover our affair? Strange, but this question, instead of frightening me, excites me.

We go to the table after Getulio's dinner bell rings from the barbecue shelter. The cook Esteva has roasted a suckling pig, which she brings already sliced on a tray. Her beans, cooked with pork tripe and jerky, are "serious business."

Hildo and Julio drag a political argument from the yard to the table.

Hildo weaves tremendous praise for Cuba, affirming that Fidel has been able to implement socialism and plant its seeds in the Caribbean, while Julio criticizes the island regime with its Castro tyranny. Carla latches onto Hildo, so they seem to be back in step with each other after some months of cold friendship. Everything indicates that it was Carla's fault for not inviting Hildo to her birthday party in this same place. Hildo is very sensitive; he does not tolerate that sort of omission, although from my perspective, what happened was probably nothing more than a glitch in communication.

I see that I am obliged to take my seat next to Julio. Poor thing. So caught up in his world, sending off blows against the Castro regime. Heloisa cites George Orwell; Hildo lights fire by invoking Marx and Gramsci; I eat my *farofa* with beans in peace. I feel like mentioning the film *L'Aveu* by Costa-Gavras, with Yves Montand, but I don't. Hildo talks nonstop, his voice echoing off the walls of the old colonial house. He roars against American imperialism, hunger, and the misery of Latin America. Let him not ruin my appetite; let my beans rest in peace.

Esteva brings milk custard and fruits from the garden for dessert. The discussion slows down as we eat and drink our coffee. Carla offers wine to help digest the pork. I accept a small glass. We get up and go to the living room to listen to Portuguese *fados*.[31] I sit down in the rocking chair ("Your brown eyes..." sings Amália Rodrigues). I think of Marcelo's brown eyes and agree to have one more glass of wine. Hildo says something about the Revolution of the Carnations[32]; Julio mentions contemporary Portuguese poetry; Carla and Heloisa sit together on the sofa; the rocking chair rocks and rocks; the wine makes me go all soft; I think about Marcelo, about brown eyes of so many different sizes; Carla tells me to go to her room, where I can fall on the bed in peace.

---

[31] *Fado*: a Portuguese song of lament, love, and sadness, often eerily sung in a wailing voice. Amália Rodrigues (1920–1999) was one of the most famous *fadistas*. Although fado is not heard much in Brazil, this sophisticated international crowd does listen to it.

[32] Revolution of the Carnations: the popular name given the April 25, 1974, military-led overthrow of the long-standing *Estado Novo* dictatorial regime in Portugal, which led shortly thereafter to the end of the hated Colonial Wars and to the independence of the country's African colonies (and East Timor), as well as to the restoration of democracy in Portugal herself.

12

Carla takes my glasses off, saying that I look good like that, and that I should use contact lenses. She slides the frames slowly off my eyes, and I feel her fingers rub against my temples. She wanted to caress my face. Carla tries my glasses to discover my degree of myopia and astigmatism. She looks funny with the kind of frame that I wear. I let out a little laugh; she smiles unpleasantly and pulls the glasses off her face.

We allow ourselves to sit quietly on the sofa with that after-lunch torpor. It was, after all, a heavy lunch. I am feeling sleepy, and Hildo Leão is napping in front of me. The record has ended, and a heavy silence hangs over the house, the cottage. Carla is smoking.

A boring argument between Hildo and Julio. It lasted through the whole meal. I defended Julio's arguments, citing Orwell's *1984*, Thomas More, and *The Republic*. This was just because I felt sorry for him, since he appeared to have been put in a corner by Hildo's rhetorical potshots. He gestured like a tribunal, and his heavy Bahian accent made it seem as if Rui Barbosa had come back to life.

Tyrant flycatchers chirp, and a horse gallops by on the road. Carla rubs her tiny hand along the sofa until it finds mine. I am taken by surprise. I feel heat on my face. I lower my eyes; I can't look at her. So that's it. Or could it be friendship, simple affection between two women? My husband is sleeping in the front bedroom. What would his reaction be if he found us holding hands on the sofa or hugging or even kissing? In my opinion, men are used to feeling jealous only of other men, not women (except Proust, who did feel it, although his "women" were not really women). I need to urgently take a lover. Hildo has made sweet eyes at me. On the other hand, I know he's crazy about Estela, that dark-haired girl in the graduate course. There's no solution. One of these nights, I'm going to the bus station, and I'll stand there making *troittoir*. They say that homosexuals pick up young soldiers there. (Could it be that Julio does those things?) Maybe I'll have the same fate.

I take my hand away from Carla's and stand up on the pretext of putting on another record. She seemed annoyed by my gesture. She picks up the bottle of wine and serves herself another glass. I'm looking for John Lennon, but it is clear that Carla's father doesn't listen to John Lennon. I put on another record of fados.

I go to the window and set my eyes on a stand of jasmine. I fear that Carla may come up and hug me from behind. She doesn't come, but I ask myself if I should continue to be her friend if she really does have other intentions. I smell the scent of the flowers and turn around, looking at the closed door of the bedroom. I push it and it opens slowly, then I go in quietly. Darkness is complete. Renato's body lies on its stomach. I lie down and hug him, but he doesn't move, only breathing, like a machine that inflates intermittently.

13

In the pauses in my typing, the music penetrates the window and makes his presence so alive that I cannot continue to write my book. I am simply typing up the manuscript, since I keep the monk-like habit of writing my own fantasies down in longhand. Although I don't have to invent anything at this moment, the guitar music bothers me desperately.

Under an uncommonly clear sky, the air habitually dry, and a sun that continues to fry the grass, I don't think of going to the park to read the newspapers, nor to the club swimming pool, but just stay home listening to the sweet music, which enchants me like the poet's lyre.

I walk nervously through the room. The sound does not stop.

On another day, I couldn't stand it, and I told Renato. He went to the Bierfass, and after a good dozen draft beers, he was still hungry and ordered spaghetti *alla carbonara.* I let everything out, that I was in love with my neighbor.

"But you don't even really know him…how can that be?" Renato rolled the spaghetti around his fork without looking at me. "Do you know what I think? It's a lack of something to do, something to think. You know, you're writing your first novel, that's true, but your love life is in a hell of a hole. Zero. I think that you just got into the business of working on your crazy book and haven't paid any attention to your love life. So you start to put junk in your head. How can someone fall in love with someone they don't even know? Careful. That's a huge obsession."

As soon as Renato ended his diagnosis, two urchins appeared from outside and asked for the remains of the meat we had munched on as an appetizer. Renato smiled. He stuck a toothpick in a little piece of the meat and held it in the air, a little bit over the heads of the boys, who suddenly raised their arms and jumped wildly to get the meat, like starving dogs. Renato was entertaining himself. I felt hatred toward him at that moment and regretted opening one of my secret doors to him. I picked up two more pieces and gave them to the boys. Flies swept through the air.

"Now tell me what it's like. Explain this: you mean you've never even spoken to the guy?" Renato was provoking me, not for any real interest he had in my sentimental novella, but rather for breaking the ice that formed between us after the street boys appeared.

I then told him that the other day, I saw the neighbor boy in the record store. I was buying a sonata for piano and violin by César Frank when he came up and asked to see the record cover. He started a conversation, saying that he loved César Frank. I got wound up. We had a long talk about classical music. He has a strange tic that causes him to sniff from time to time and to cough. He said good-bye quickly and fled from the store.

From then on, whenever we happen to cross at the entrance or the elevator, we talk a little about classical music. He loves the Baroque period. He doesn't like Romanticism or contemporary music. Mozart's last symphonies for him are an insult, a discrepancy, and he twisted his nose when I mentioned my love of Mahler.

"And César Frank?"

Luciano limited himself to smiling and shrugging his shoulders. Such are human contradictions.

I think destiny (and I'm a fatalist to a certain extent) has brought about unexpected encounters between us. I saw Luciano at the National Theater during the intermission of a concert. They were presenting a rather crude version of Mozart's *Requiem*. He was alone, and I was with a lady librarian friend who introduced me to the conductor's wife and an acquaintance dressed and coiffed in an extravagant manner, a woman from the state of Goiás and married to a guy who got rich in the early days of Brasilia. She commented while I was looking at Luciano from the corner of my eyes:

"Oh, this *Lacrimosa* makes me so excited…"

I excused myself to go to the bathroom, and, on the way back, I intercepted Luciano and asked if he had enjoyed the first part. He made a face of disgust. Then we prolonged the conversation.

After the concert, I took leave of my ladies and invited Luciano to have a beer with me at Fritz's. He accepted.

"So you have already gone out together?"

Renato now seems to be paying more attention to my story.

He told me that he had gone into architecture, because he had a certain talent for drawing, and his father, an engineer, had encouraged him. But what he really likes is music. He had played electric guitar in a rock band in São Paulo three years before. Then he opened his ears to classical music and the possibilities of the guitar in that field. He had fallen in love with Narciso Yepes and Paco de Lucia.

"Do you plan to play professionally someday?"

Luciano made a face, as if to say "you never know."

I talked a little bit about myself. He wanted to know about this business of literary style, whether I chose a mode of writing or the words just flowed normally. I told him that I liked what I used to write better when I was younger than what I do now. He was surprised. Today, with my accumulated reading, after a reflection on literature, studies, classes, and theoretical bibliography, I really think I have moved away from my original style, or at least from that old and almost naïve "purity" that made my first writing sound more authentic. Luciano didn't show any reaction.

The waiter brought plates of salmon and herring paste, which he devoured voraciously. He told me that he had been fat as a child ("Me, too," I said), that he had had to go on a diet with a doctor, and that everything began when he suffered indigestion at a Sunday lunch with his parents at a buffet restaurant. Luciano still has vestiges of his once robust physique.

Renato was no longer paying any attention to what I was telling him. He must be thinking about his most recent lover, that girl studying at the CEUB.[33] I had also been drinking too much, and I now capped all the drafts I had had that afternoon with a *steinhäger*.

It was dark.

With some effort, Renato and I got up from the Bierfass.

---

[33] CEUB: the Centro de Ensino Unificado de Brasilia or the Center of Unified Teaching of Brasilia, a private university founded in 1968.

"Are you okay to drive, dude?"

"Of course, of course," I said, and I continued staggering to my VW.

I was certain that I was driving toward Medici Bridge, but, suddenly, I realized that I was on the Brasilia-Belo Horizonte highway, surrounded by violent traffic of cars and trucks. Frightened, I looked for the turnabout sign. I found it. The VW had to move in a zigzag. Suddenly, I found myself in the Embassy Sector. Shit, what am I doing here? I put it in reverse and wanted to make a U-turn, but I hit the curb. I entered a dead-end alley. The doorman of one of the embassies is going to think that I am, at a minimum, a terrorist, but when I found my Quad, I thanked Saint Christopher for the ride he gave me on his shoulders, because that's the only way I could have made it to the North Wing.

14

It hurt so much. Heloisa even hid it. She was delicate; she didn't pull her hand away quickly; she simply slid it away from mine. It was as if the silence were threatening to saturate the air that we breathe, making it suffocating. Heloisa knelt down and chose a record from the shelf. My hand continued immobile for a time, just as she had left it abandoned on the sofa. I hold it like that, because it still contains the warmth of her skin. I'm not going to bring it close to me; I want Heloisa to see it just as she left it—with the palm up and my fingers spread, waiting.

The music spills off the record. I like the one she chose. We have similar tastes in music, one of our affinities. But Heloisa did not come back to sit with me on the sofa; she went to the window to look out at the yard. Naturally, she calls me; she wants me to approach and embrace her from the back and—who knows?—soften her face with a kiss. No. I've already dared too much for today. I advanced too far into slippery ground for me to try to violate her again. There are gestures that we do with difficulty, but which are definitive. For example, I have just announced my love for Heloisa with a simple linking of fingers. And how soft her hand is…. In the meantime, she didn't say a word. I don't believe that the act of getting up, putting on a record that I like, and going to the window really means rejection. If it did, she would have acted surprised and said with a certain amount of fright, "What is this, Carla!" No, it was gentle of her to look for a record, and then contemplate the yard, as if waiting for me.

All a matter of patience.

(Damn hope that keeps us hypnotized, holding onto the same purposes, until reality destroys it.)

I take a swallow of my wine.

Heloisa moves away from the window. She doesn't dare look at me, and she seems sad. She slides her little hand over the door to the room where Renato is sleeping. Could that gesture already have said everything she had to tell me? Should I lay down my arms, surrender, and spill tears on the battlefield? No. I am excited by the game. Renato doesn't like her—that's obvious. He doesn't show any affection, any tender look at all for her. Heloisa is suffering. The other day, my cruelty got to the point of my asking her if she ever thought of having a child. Heloisa blushed, embarrassed, and said, "Not for now." I laughed inside. I spoke with Julio about Renato, and we both agreed on the same point. Still, I want to keep him as a friend.

They woke up (could it be that Heloisa really slept?) and prepared to leave. "I'm staying," I said. In the dark of night, I heard the noise of the car moving off, and I put on the record again that she had chosen. I served myself a whiskey on the rocks and listened to music until sleep came.

The next day, Mom and Dad arrive, and later, Ricardo with his girlfriend. Dad and I drink beer in the yard, right there in the sun where I had lain with Heloisa. Dad talks about work. I change the subject to Renato, praising him greatly, and I explain that he wants to be promoted in the ministry. Dad scratches his chin. Mom appears all misty in her gauze dress and sits down with us. The senator certainly will not be giving me an immediate answer, but I know very well how to treat him. I'll check back with him in a week. Renato will be eternally grateful to me.

15

The problem is that now, I'm beginning to feel sick. At first, it's easier to tolerate. Later on, it gets harder. The features and working-class attitudes of Marcelo have become alarmingly clear. And there's no way. If I tell Julio, he'll come on with that elitism of his. Elitism shit. There's no way. Once a hard nose, always a hard nose. Marcelo is good-looking, nice, but he has terrible taste in clothes, music, movies, and only God knows what else. These little things affect our relationship. That habit, for example, of saying "location" instead of "place" drives me crazy. No, I can't stand bad taste. Heloisa, at least, usually shows good taste. The other day, Marcelo practically obliged me to go to a show by a crappy local rock singer who exasperates me. I almost left at intermission. Besides, I don't like being seen with him in public at all. If anyone runs into me or tells Heloisa, Marcelo is, for all effects, my cousin." My cousin from Brasilia, son of Aunt So-and-So and Uncle Such-and-Such, who are not really my uncle and aunt, but rather cousins of my mother, who have been living here a long time, don't you remember, Heloisa? You never pay attention to what I say. Right after we got to Brasilia, I looked them up and went to eat with them in the military Quad in the South Wing. You still hadn't come, don't you remember, Heloisa?"

Our encounters must be limited to the motel at kilometer X on the Brasilia-Belo Horizonte highway. He insists that we go to the Beirut, but I resist stubbornly. In the first place, I detest that bar and its clientele, people who look like dirty, lowlife hippies.

I talked to Julio about my affair with the "girl student from CEUB." I didn't have the courage to reveal the whole truth to him. I felt obligated to put my friend in costume to protect the image that Julio has of me. Someday, I'll tell him everything, but I need more time. I think that if Julio knew that I was a fellow traveler, he would get excited, and, without meaning to, would fill me with advice gained from his vast experience in this area.

The last time was in that restaurant at the lake. We drank beer and more beer. Julio told me about his obsession with his neighbor. He calls it passion, but I correct him, calling it an obsession, a word I consider more suitable. We ordered a serving of jerky. There was a cool breeze coming off the lake. Julio likes Heloisa, and he naturally advised me to break up with the student from the CEUB.

"I don't know...she gives me the best turn-on. Screwing her takes me to glory..."

From spending so much time with Julio, I end up using his expressions. There was no one else in the restaurant, and we didn't have lunch, we just drank beer and nibbled on the jerky. The breeze turned into a wind, and we began shivering from cold, until I had the brilliant idea of grabbing a cloth off one of the tables and wrapping myself up in it. Julio immediately imitated my gesture. The two of us then remained wrapped up in the tablecloths, drinking our last beers, without being seen by the waiters who had gone inside for shelter while the sunset turned the waters of the lake red.

When I got home, I asked Heloisa to fry me some eggs. I almost fell asleep hearing the unintelligible sounds of the television mixed with the hissing of butter boiling in the frying pan. Heloisa brought me the eggs mixed with rice, which I ate in just a few forksful.

"Did you want to have a child, Heloisa?"

She blushed, bent her head to the side, and didn't say anything. I insisted and she said a shy "yes." I picked up her hand, kissed it, dragged her close to me, and hugged her. Then I asked her to turn the TV off. We went to the bedroom. We began to caress each other, until I felt a desire for what Heloisa always refuses to do. I ran my tongue along her whole back with the intention of having her give in. Nothing doing. She kneeled at the foot of the bed and cried. I waited impassively for her to stop. Pretending to be naïve, and treating the matter with utmost normality, I asked her why she had that reaction. I saw then that she was drawing close to me again, and I embraced her. Heloisa finally gave in; that way, she imagined our marriage would be preserved. This is certainly not the way to have children, but I have had an uncontrollable desire for some time to practice that variation with my wife. Heloisa complained at first, then gave in gently like a slave who acknowledges her punishment.

16

It hurt, but I submitted to his desire.

17

Grilo Falante calls me up and invites me to go out. I was in a bad mood, exactly like on one of my first days here a cloudy Saturday morning, when I was sitting at the little desk trying to read *Père Goriot*. I couldn't get past the first line of a chapter when the doorbell rang. It was Grilo Falante, who, with his noisy presence, immediately made me feel better. I offered him some domestic vodka with lime and ice.

"How people drink here in Brasilia! Any house you go to, it's always, 'Will you have a little whiskey? How about a beer?' and we end up drinking like mad."

He took me out to lunch. It was the first time I'd been to Fritz's, which had just opened its doors and still didn't have much variety on its menu. I chose a goulash, and the afternoon I spent with Grilo swept away my sadness.

I laugh a lot with him. In spite of the fact that he stutters, he talks with surprising speed. Very thin, agitated, he gesticulates by raising his small hands. He has crooked teeth, which he shows whenever he has trouble getting the words out of his mouth.

Well, he came to save me yesterday from another deep depression.

"I was feeling kind of bad today…."

"Let's go downtown. Now, now, come on!"

I put on a Lee jacket that I wear on these cool July nights, and we take the VW toward the bus station. It was a Wednesday, a day off for the soldiers based in the capital. I parked the car, scratched and dented in its battles against the sea and storms, in front of the brightly lit shopping center. We entered and wandered around like hungry cats through the galleries. Soldiers went by in groups, some in street clothes, but easy to identify. People were looking in still lit-up store windows and at movie posters. We went up the escalator. On the second floor, the video game places emit noises like a carnival, an amusement park. Recruits and big boys go around. The noise of those infernal lighted machines! Grilo Falante calls me to drink a beer in a little bar next to the source of that noise. Who should appear but Aparicio Gama, who works in the ministry with Grilo with his nervous blue Gloria Swanson eyes. He sits with us, in spite of the natural difficulty of his extremely tight jeans, and when he says he is reading the memoires of D. Isabel de Orleans e Bragança, the Countess of Paris,[34] he recites a discourse in favor of the restoration of the monarchy in Brazil. Grilo, who defines himself as a man of the Left, replies with indignation, citing the ignominy of slavery and the patent social injustice of monarchical regimes of the past. Since it didn't seem the right time for arguments of this sort, I commented that time was passing. Immediately, Aparicio took his leave. We paid the bill and resumed our trip through the hallways of the mall. Deep inside, I felt fear—that fear of all unknown situations and those that are still to take place—and tedium in that futile search.

"Do you think it is easy? You have to take a stand!"

Grilo likes to unearth old expressions.

I am surprised by two figures, mine and Grilo's, reflected in a store window.

We go down to the ground floor, leave the mall, and cross the street in the direction of the upper level of the bus station. There Grilo greets a boy in uniform, good-looking, with heavy eyebrows almost grown together.

"Hi, Caio! How are you doing?"

He and Grilo seem to be long-time acquaintances. My friend introduces me to his friend who shakes my hand. It feels heavy and rough. Grilo invites him to take a ride with us. I continue to feel somewhat wary in the car and wonder which one will be best served tonight. Caio says he is hungry, and I think of taking him to a restaurant, but Grilo insists I drive to the nearest fast food place. I park and the boy gets out.

---

[34] D. Isabel de Orleans e Bragança, the Countess of Paris (1911–2003): the great-granddaughter of D. Pedro II. She spent most of her life in Europe involved in charity matters. Her two-volume memoires were called *De todo coração* (*Tout m'est bonheur*).

"Are you crazy to take a recruit to a restaurant? Besides the danger of being seen by somebody we know, you don't want to spend a fortune on the guy."

Caio comes back with a sandwich, which he devours in a minute.

"Let's go to the house!" orders Grilo, as if I were his coachman.

In my friend's apartment, Caio throws his cap on a chair and removes his green jacket, showing the name of his unit on his tee shirt. He sits on the sofa between the two of us. Grilo puts Dalva de Oliveira[35] on the record player and serves us a whiskey. I am visibly shaken. Grilo then begins to caress Caio's thorax, and Caio then pulls up his shirt to show his trained military muscles. I notice a tiny tattoo in the shape of a butterfly on the boy's brown biceps. As a first step in my approach, I try to kiss it. He shows no reaction. Grilo's grin looks like that of a sneaky rat in a cartoon, the one that gnaws unseen on the cheese. Thus, he opens the front of Caio's green pants and hunts for his penis, which he begins to manipulate. For my part, I continue to smooth over Caio's arms and chest. Suddenly, he gets up and says:

"I want to take a bath."

"Go on, you first," the host says, as soon as Caio leaves the living room.

There I went, and there I was: a docile horse of the Spartan horseman.

---

[35] Dalva de Oliveira (1917–1972): Brazilian singer from the heyday of radio.

18

I couldn't take it anymore. I had to say something. Days and days went by without her calling. I didn't call her either, out of stubbornness. I came very close to dialing her number. I decided to confess everything all at once, since sometimes a blast of cold water is better than slow cooking on low heat. Yesterday, I walked into the Department of History offices, a horribly hot, dry day, and found Heloisa reading a book. I stopped in front of her as she raised her eyes and looked at me very surprised. She didn't say anything; she just continued to look at me through the lenses of her slightly crooked glasses. I couldn't stand that situation, so I turned my back to her and hustled out of there.

19

The drought got worse. I breathe in cold air that threatens to hurt my nostrils, as what usually happens during these months of August and September. The night is clear, promising another sunny day tomorrow. After three months, we are getting tired of so much blue sky, and we look forward to the rains. Just the first drops will turn the grass green.

After work, the thought of getting home and finding Heloisa sent me off to the sauna at the Hotel Nacional. I called to tell her that I wouldn't be having dinner. As soon as I entered the sort of party room that is the bar, I met up with Guedes. Shit! I didn't expect to see anyone from the office. Inevitably, there would be boring little talk about the ministry. Guedes is a zealous bureaucrat, efficient and boring.

"It was necessary to find just the right legal term. We have to improve the forms, the terminology, in order to get exactly the right sense. Without precise phrasing, the text goes off and is ineffective…"

I ordered a whiskey at the bar.

"The happiest days of my life are those in which I leave the office and feel like I have written a really good memo. A clean, perfect communication."

What Guedes is looking for would be, platonically speaking, the Memorandum on the Plane of Ideas.

Guedes's skin is earth-colored, and he has several tires on his belly.

"Guedes, why don't you get some exercise? You could play tennis with me at the club."

It may seem contradictory, but Guedes loves to drive fast. He has an Alfa Romeo that shoots around the Esplanade. He makes it to Rio in ten hours; he almost flies, and he dreams about the perfect memorandum.

I finish my whiskey, get away from Guedes, and go into the steam sauna. The mist hides fat bodies, lowered heads, and nervous legs, made uncomfortable by the heat. The smell of eucalyptus at first gives an impression of cleanliness, freshness, but after a few seconds, it seems like suffocation. Some peer through the spyglass of the door. I'm standing, since all the spots on the brick seats are taken. Sweating buckets, I leave and get under a cold shower. (Funny—Julio told me that Grilo Falante fainted once in the shower due to a sudden loss of blood pressure.)

I go back to the bar, praying not to run into Guedes—but, by luck, I know that he never misses his dinner hour—and who should I meet? Julio.

"What a coincidence! Do you know I was thinking about you?"

"No fooling," says Julio, and he offers to drink a whiskey with me.

Julio begins to talk about literature. He asks me if I have read Lucio Cardoso's book yet, which he lent to Heloisa a couple of months ago. "No, I haven't read it. I haven't had time, Julio. I'm so involved in this business of the student from CEUB that I haven't had my head in place to do anything." Julio always talks about that guy. "I don't know. I really don't like Brazilian literature very much. I distrust it a bit, and I find Machado de Assis[36] a tremendous pain in the ass. I like Hemingway, Henry Miller..." Julio looks at me with disdain, changes the subject, and goes back to telling me about his obsession with his neighbor. I confess that I am really tired of that story, and that I still fail to understand how someone can fall in love with an image, an object only known from the outside.

"Forget about him, buddy," I say. "You have to remember that that guy is just like you, me, or anyone. He craps and farts just like anyone else."

Julio returns a look, as if to say, "What vulgar advice, Renato..." I'm a terrible counselor—I have no gift for psychology. Julio invites

---

[36] Joaquim Maria Machado de Assis (1839–1908): arguably the greatest literary figure in Brazil, and one of the very finest in the Portuguese language. He is best known for his short stories and novels. A self-educated mulatto who rose from poverty, he was the first president of the Brazilian Academy of Letters.

me to have dinner, but I impose two conditions: one, don't spill praise for Lucio Cardoso; two, don't mention the neighbor again.

"Grilo is right. Pick up some recruit, fall in love with him, support him if necessary, but never be a voyeur of a neighbor, Julio, for the love of God." I return to my role as a counselor with my coat slung over my back, hanging from a single finger, looking for my car in the parking lot, my hair still wet and feeling fresh from the sauna.

We go to the Tarantella and empty two bottles of Chilean white wine as we talk about stupid things. Julio tells me a crude story about him and Grilo having shared a young soldier recently. I pretend I don't think it's funny, then he asks me about Heloisa.

Then I decide (I don't really know if the drunk decide anything) to reveal to Julio the true identify of my affair with that CEUB student. He appeared neither shocked nor satisfied as I had hoped. He just looked at me from the depth of his eyes.

"But I'm going to end it. I'm tired of it. To tell the truth, I think he's in poor taste, you know? Kind of possessive, too."

"When you stop liking someone, his defects really jump out at you," Julio philosophizes.

We pay the slightly inflated bill, and Julio tries to convince me to go to the Beirut for a nightcap. It doesn't take much to convince a drunk to have another shot.

The Beirut is sadly empty on Tuesday. A few couples with curly hair and wearing leather sandals are talking over bottles of beer. Julio, who always takes a long time to find a parking spot, comes down the street at his customary pace. I tell him about the novel I'm writing. He seems to give intermittent signs of interest and boredom. I don't want to tire him out with my literary efforts, but he's the only friend who I can confess my imaginings to.

"Wow! Could it be raining?" He changed the subject. "I thought I felt a few drops."

"Impossible. It's still too soon to rain."

Julio was right. A bolt of lightning scratches the sky; it thunders. But the rain does not fall. These are the warning signs of the new season. After the third "nightcap," I call on Julio to go to Aquarius, the only "understanding" night club in Brasilia. He opens his eyes wide.

Aquarius—I didn't even know just how to get there, but Julio directed me there, taking the role of a *Virgilio candango*. It's in the basement of a semi-abandoned shopping center, which makes its customers call it "the hole," a nickname completely compatible with the looks of the place—a smoky, dirty ditch. A black guy with a shirt that is too short is leaning against the wall at the foot of the stairs. Young soldiers, prostitutes, transvestites, drunks, and bums wander through the little bars on that underground level. I have the impression that everybody is probably carrying knives and razors in their belts, socks, and even teeth. The smoke makes it hard to see into that little hell where an enormous black guy is holding guard and selling tickets.

This kind of place, however, excites me. There are wooden boards set over the entrance due to construction. We enter and descend some steps. There is a water fountain there with an angel in the corner, the lights tending toward red, and dry ice invades the dance floor upon which the music gives great hammering blows. On Tuesday night, there was hardly anybody there. A queer who looks like an Indian dances in the beam of light. Julio goes to the bar and leans against the counter, ordering two gin and tonics for us. Suddenly, I get a crazy desire to get out of here. What the heck did I do to come here to this gay den of iniquity? I spin the ice with lemon in the tall cup. I take a gulp. I look at the bright globe with boredom, and I whisper a supposedly funny comment in Julio's ear. Now he knows everything. He knows my secret. He should be drooling with joy. Is he going to come down on top of me, or simply release the reins on a secret attraction that I suspect he has for me? No, Julio likes me as a friend, just a friend. Here is the problem of human relations: we never know exactly what others think of us, especially because that hidden feeling is so changeable, so fluid, that even the other person often cannot define it precisely.

I tap Julio on the shoulder. "Shall we go?"

"Just a little longer," he answers.

Suddenly, a song I like comes on, and a boy appears in the fumes of dry ice. Lights and sound outline his features. His black eyes have a deep brilliance.

"So, you want to go now?"

"Just a little longer," I say, repeating his last words.

I go sit on the sofa at the edge of the dance floor. The boy with blondish hair approaches. The gin is gone, but I don't want to move away from him to go get another at the bar. Julio then says good-bye; he's bored and tired. I don't know how to talk to the boy; I've never done a pickup at a bar. Julio must have left this den with a contented smile on his face, the shithead. After all, I'm a queer just like him. Damn him. I confessed because I wanted to.

"You like a drink?"

He nods his head, and I go get two gin and tonics and make small talk. The dance floor is completely empty. I take the boy's hand.

Outside, I see that the skin of his face is rippled by pimples. It would be better for him to live in the dark parts of the club. We cross the better lit mall, get to the parking lot, and to my car.

"Where would you like to go?"

"I don't know," he answers.

I don't ask his name; I don't feel like knowing. Nor does he ask mine. Maybe we'll go to a motel, since I hate to fuck in the car. I drive to City Park. I stop in a parking lot surrounded by pine trees. The boy begins to suck me. I pull down his pants, and we screw right there, hardly moving on the seats, under the supervision of the trees in the park. The night is cool and a damp wind is blowing, foreshadowing rain. We both smile.

I leave him on the W-3.

The Axis is deserted. I don't feel drunk anymore. I barely drive, and the white lights cut across my windshield. The mute buildings sit at the edges of the Central Axis, the bureaucratic population sleeping happily and with their bellies full to wake up ready the next day. I follow the long road, and I feel a numbness putting my arms to sleep, my legs, my whole body. I see the signs on the superquads, the empty bus station, the North Wing, and it seems that I am sinking deeply into an endless voyage. A flash appears on the horizon, and the first drops of rain sprinkle onto the windshield. It is the new season announcing itself.

THE RAINS

1

The senator's jovial face appears on the giant screen in black and white. At that time, he was much younger. It's funny how old people's smiles are different from those of younger people. Maybe I'm just imagining it, but could it be that his face radiated a naïve hope, and now what I see is nothing more than a kind of complacent and conforming expression? In the home movies, you can see the brilliant shine of the senator's eyes, while today, after turning the lights on, you see only his wrinkled face showing a pair of dim-lit eyes.

The movie ends, all the film having passed from one reel to the other, and a square of yellow light appears on the wall. Just as in the theatre, voices rise. They are excited, laughing and talking about the film, really just family scenes spliced together. They were at a picnic at the Alto da Boa Vista in Rio, on an empty Barra da Tijuca,[37] or at their country home in Teresópolis.[38] I see Carla—small, always plump with her round face—accompanied by her brothers, playing *peteca*[39] on the beach or making faces to the camera.

The senator drinks his whiskey and converses with Renato; that is, Renato listens to him because the senator gives a monologue. I am upset, as I see my husband playing the role of a brownnoser. He is so proud at home, and apparently at work, too. How he appears diminished, begging for a job in the department with greater prestige

---

[37] Barra da Tijuca, or just "Barra": the southernmost beach in Rio, until the 1970s, a pristine and almost uninhabited outpost. Now it is highly developed with hotels, apartments, malls, and congestion.

[38] Teresópolis: a community in the mountains west of Rio and a favorite place for vacation homes and weekend getaways.

[39] *Peteca*: a game akin to badminton but played with a "hand shuttlecock," which resembles a large badminton shuttlecock or bird, but without a racket. This game is of indigenous origin.

and a few more bucks in his pocket every month. It's demeaning to see what he is putting up with. His eyes shine, and he smiles to the senator who is tasting his scotch. In private, Renato spoke badly about the senator and Carla, saying that he is bionic, a bootlicker to the military, and with no professional ability, while the daughter is inopportune, in need of attention, and cloying. Really, Carla has stepped up her visits to us. It seems like she has hardly left our home in recent months. And I have already noticed the bad mood Renato gets into whenever she shows up. Well, he's right. We have the right to be alone, to have time just to ourselves. I think that's why Renato doesn't stay home anymore. He knows that when he comes in, who will be there? Carla.

She just appears, and I don't have any way to give her an excuse and claim another commitment. She comes and stays for lunch, for dinner. Carla sits on the sofa with me and doesn't stop talking. Her conversation is pleasant enough, and, in the midst of all the monotony of life in this city, I let myself be carried away by her rhythmic voice. Sometimes I don't even listen, but she has a soft way of telling stories that almost rocks me to sleep. Carla has a habit of adjusting the frames of her glasses, and she smokes one cigarette after another. White strands are appearing prematurely in her hair.

"No, I had to go to work. I had to. I couldn't sit still in this little life that we have here. To spend all day locked in a superquad would drive me crazy," I say.

"Yes, as soon as Father was elected, I had to move here. What would I do in Rio? But I had to find a job. Sitting around doing nothing wouldn't work. So I found a place at the ministry."

"But do you plan to work at the ministry your whole life?"

"Well, the ministry is my job. Painting, as you know, is my profession."

Carla's painting: she makes some collages, and then inserts paintings and drawings. Some pictures remind one of Paul Klee because of a certain playful atmosphere. Carla studied art in Paris. Once in a while, with a fearful smile, she shows me a recently painted picture and asks my opinion, but I cannot, I simply cannot, talk to her frankly. I am afraid of hurting her; I am afraid of hurting her a lot, for example, by mentioning her impromptu visit to my office at the university. I confess my failure to understand such an absurd event.

Renato, halfway "high," suddenly got up excitedly to tell some story that he thinks will be funny to the senator, but seeing the old man's uncomfortable expression, he sat down, embarrassed. The two start their conversation again, pausing, speaking formally, and I can no longer stand to stay here with nothing to talk about with Mrs. Senator, who is wearing a thin dress. I have already praised the home movies, their house in Teresópolis, and all their children. The oldest really is good-looking.

"What thunder!" says the senator's wife, frightened.

"But it's not raining, just threatening."

I had barely finished making this meteorological affirmation with great assurance when rain broke out. It was the first after months and months of drought.

The rain kept us at the senator's house longer. Flashes of lightning light up the large windows of the living room while thunder blasts our ears, and the sound of rain seems interminable, refreshing the ground. Carla, reclining on the salmon-colored sofa, doesn't stop looking at me between puffs on her cigarette. An oblique light from a floor lamp shines on her face. That's how she massages my ego.

2

It started off cold today, and the rain beat hard outside, inviting me to laze between the sheets. So I stayed in bed doing the *grasse matineé* until eleven. I stretched out like a cat, and when I raised the shade, I saw Luciano down below changing a tire on his car. He was soaked from the rain. I leaned out on the sill and thought of shouting to him to offer my help—I who have absolutely no mechanical skills—but I gave up and went to make my coffee. I came back and saw that Luciano was still at the back of the building, struggling with the tire, the jack, and the nuts. Why would he insist on changing the tire today in this storm? His hair is wet and disheveled.

I take up my book again; that is, I type the chapter that I wrote last night. For days, I've felt like destroying everything; so great is my discouragement over the story and its treatment. I detect too many influences, unnecessary passages, ridiculous observations, empty characters. So then I decide to rewrite it from scratch. No. I reread it and conclude that I should continue from the point where I had left off. *Navegar é preciso,* one must navigate.[43]

The doorbell rings and interrupts me. It is Pedro, my neighbor from upstairs. I made coffee for him, and we chatted. Pedro told me that he talked with his boyfriend yesterday. He lives in Rio Grande do Sul,[44] Pedro's home state. He came to Brasilia somewhat against his will because of his job. He is an attorney. He met the guy just weeks before moving here and fell in love, but it was impossible to cancel his transfer with his company, since the process was already underway.

---

[43] An expression supposedly used by old Portuguese explorers and consecrated in the poem of the same name by Fernando Pessoa.

[44] Rio Grande do Sul: southernmost state in Brazil, bordering Uruguay, Argentina, and Paraguay. It is known for its peculiar *gaúcho* culture, as well as its Spanish, German, and Italian influences from immigration and border contact.

Poor guy. Anyway, it wouldn't look good to his bosses if he wanted to renege on the move. Since his arrival, he has satisfied his longing by telephone. Thanks to Alexander Graham Bell.

After his call, Pedro hasn't been able to sleep, so he takes pills. In a dresser drawer, he keeps boxes and more boxes of pills, which he can buy. Thanks to prescriptions provided by a doctor friend of his. I normally go off to sleep by drinking four or five doses of whiskey, but Pedro doesn't drink. He is blond and nervous. His hands shake as he smokes, and he has a way of fiddling with his watchband.

He says he likes the guy from the south a lot. His name is Inocencio (what a shitty name!), and he is a psychologist. They plan to marry someday. I suggest a church in Amsterdam. He doesn't laugh. He says his guy never betrays him, just as he himself has lived like a nun. "Like a Barefoot Carmelite," I say, but Pedro doesn't think it's very funny. Deep inside, I don't believe in loyalty. Not even I am capable of such abnegation, I who profess the courtly love of the troubadours, like a Lancelot. Didn't you see, Julinho, my love, how you openly cheated on Luciano with Caio the soldier? (This time Pedro laughs.)

After having a nice lunch of fish with Pedro at a restaurant in the North Wing, I take a nap, and then go back to my book. I type one page, and the telephone rings. It's Gastão Abrantes, my colleague at the university and a professor of philosophy. He invites me to have a beer at the Beirut.

Fat, bearded, and wearing glasses, with his hands swinging in a rowing motion as he takes lumbering steps, Gastão looks like a philosopher that Aristophanes would not hesitate to lift up over his *Clouds*. We go in his caramel-colored Fiat, while he complains about his students' mediocrity and the rain that has soaked the capital. As we approach the Beirut, he changes the subject to something less prosaic, like Nietzsche. He says he is engrossed in the thought of the German from Basel. He expounds with explanations about the *birth of the tragedy in the spirit of music* and the Apollonian and Dionysian concepts.

At the table, we met other professors and—who would have guessed?—my neighbor Luciano. I feel disoriented but force myself to listen to Gastão's lessons on Nietzsche. Gastão moves his face close and twists his mustache as he speaks.

I try to get a conversation going with Luciano.

"I saw you changing your tire today in the rain."

He smiles, and someone says, "In that building, everyone knows about everyone else's life."

Suddenly, Luciano invites me to a guitar jam session at his house on Saturday. I tremble. Gastão gets lost in digressions about the Dionysian power of music.

3

She calls to say that she is going to spend a few days in Rio. I say, yes, yes, sometimes that is necessary, and she hangs up when what I wanted to do was beg her to stay, since spending two weeks without seeing her is real torture.

I made coffee and try to finish a painting. I can't do it. No combination of colors seems right to me; no brush stroke seems to give the proper touch.

Father invites me to lunch today in that restaurant in the South Business Sector, where they serve a great stew on Wednesday.

He asks me why I am so interested in helping Renato, insinuating a love affair with him. Inside, I find it funny and leave the mystery floating in the air, without revealing anything, without delivering my intentions to him on a silver platter.

4

I get a call at night from Mom in Rio, saying she urgently needs to see me. Renato won't be there, so I can talk to her freely. Her voice sounded nervous, as if begging me. The boy left her. Well, sooner or later, this was going to happen anyway. It was just a matter of time. Mom didn't give me any details, just insisting on my presence. Funny—when I needed her advice, she seemed impatient and told me to put up with Renato's absences. At any rate, I'll speak to him in the morning, and then take the first shuttle flight to Rio.

In the morning, in the breakfast nook, I speak with Jucineia about my sudden trip. She pours the hot milk into my cup and complains about life. She talks about her children, her ex-husband, and the violence in Ceilândia. The other day, there was a shoot-out between the police and a local citizen. Two men were shot, and her youngest son saw it all. The child is so sensitive that he didn't talk for days. His older sister had to tear him out of the empty lot where the bodies had been laid out, because the boy was motionless, unable even to blink.

Every day, Jucineia tells me about terrible misfortunes. Listening to her is like hearing a crime program on the radio. Maybe worse. Her husband left her with three children, two girls and a boy, and never came around again. They share a shack with an old woman and her daughter in a big slum on the outskirts of the capital. I never go there.

Renato sits at the table. He still hasn't shaved, and he holds his hands to his face. His sleepy eyes barely look at me, but, certainly, they give him a special charm. He answers me by mumbling sounds with his mouth closed as he stirs sugar into his coffee and milk. He agrees to check on the price of the ticket. I make some comment to him about his dress shirts, and he simply agrees.

As I get up ("I have to do my makeup"), I can't resist running my fingers through his hair. Renato doesn't move a muscle.

5

I go along the Big Axis at night. As I go toward the bus station, the car hits a huge puddle left by the rain that fell at six o'clock this afternoon.

6

The usual break after lunch in the department. I read a super boring book about literary theory for the class that I'll be giving shortly. Hildo Leão, in front of me, reads newspapers, Fabinho reads Bataille, Gastão Abrantes slumbers in the old vinyl chair, and Ida Maria, a professor of Classical Greek, makes faces in a tiny mirror in the lid of her powder compact as she retouches her makeup.

A fly comes through the window, a victim of the heat, which will certainly bring rain by late afternoon, and it goes and buzzes around Abrantes's red, potato-shaped nose. The fat man wrinkles his face and tries to scare the insect away without opening his eyes. Hildo gives a little laugh, followed by Fabinho. The fly insists on its target and weaves spirals over Gastão's semi-bald head. Ida Maria, now a rejuvenated woman, notices the impertinence of the insect against the philosophy professor's pleasant siesta.

"What a bother!" she exclaims.

Zzzz, the fly attacks. Gastão opens his blue eyes wide, slaps the air, and then hits the paneled wall.

"What the hell!" he grunts.

The fly disappears. Gastão returns to his nap. Fabinho chats with Ida Maria about the origin of the word *poetry: poesia, poiesis.*

"But in the Poundian meaning of the thing…"

"In what meaning?" Ida Maria is taken aback by the enigmatic word.

"In the meaning of Pound, the way Ezra Pound saw the thing; that is, the root of *poieses*, making *poieses*, construction, the work that he would achieve. In analytic terms, what he is going to dismember in that stroke of *melopeia, logopeia,* and *phanopeia.*"

Ida Maria narrows her eyes.

"Does the professor have an obligation to know Pound, Fabinho?" Hildo interrupts.

"What do you mean I don't know him? Of course I do. And then you asked me a question! Do you want to hear the answer, or do you intend to teach me a lesson?"

Fabinho responds with his little laugh of a satisfied hyena. Hildo's laughter can be heard resounding out loud, even when he tries to suppress it.

The fly attacks again, and Gastão slaps his hands together in a whack! That interrupts the argument.

"Listen, I need to prepare my class," I ask.

Spirits calm down. Ida opens her powder case again and looks at herself in the mirror. Hildo and Fabinho go back to their reading.

Then the fly launches a furious attack, like a kamikaze airplane, on the mustache and resonant lips of Gastão, who suddenly jumps from the chair and slaps the air repeatedly at the insistent projectile.

"What shit!" says Gastão as he moves his head.

"Professor Abrantes!" says Ida, blushing.

Fabinho, Hildo, and I break into laughter.

Gastão complains about the number of flies in the city, gives up on his nap, and sets about grading tests. Fabinho closes his book on Bataille and picks up a volume of Foucault.

"It's a zoo—everybody is an imbecile, and no one even knows how to write in Portuguese," mumbles Gastão, shaking his old fountain pen in the air.

"When do you plan to give your course again in mythology, Ida?" I ask.

"I don't know yet," she answers dryly, with her eyes fixed on the mirror.

"Well, I fell like sitting in on it. Jung talks a lot about the mythological universe as the basis for the notion of archetypes of the collective subconscious."

"Jung is a psychoanalyst of the right, and Reich of the left!"

"What's that, Hildo?" Even Gastão Abrantes opened his eyes wide and raised his pen.

"What a Manichaean concept. Shit!" exclaims Fabinho behind his dark glasses, separating the two strands of hair falling down his forehead.

"What strange handwriting," says Ida Maria as she leans slightly to the left and glances at the stack of papers that Gastão has under his nose.

"Strange?" the professor repeats at the judgment made of his calligraphy.

"It looks like the writing of an American."

"Hold on, Ida, that's too much…an American's handwriting, indeed![42]

---

[42] Brazilians are usually much better trained in cursive than the Americans, so that their handwriting tends to be neater. [except if said Americans are parochial-school graduates!!!!!]

7

One week without Heloisa. I can't stay at home. I call friends. I go to the movies, the theater, clubs, little parties. Finally I get bored. This weekend, I got in the car and went out to the country house to paint. I set the easel up in the garden. I cut out figures from magazines. But nothing happened. I ended up eating Getulio's sausage with beer, and then drinking wine to the sound of the music that we like to listen together.

Today, I invited Julio to dinner. I found him dressed in a red poncho at home. We drank a whiskey and went to the Tarantella. Julio told me the story of his romance novel. Nothing special: a case of adolescent love like millions of others written about in the past. I like Julio's poetry, but not his prose.

We emptied two bottles of red wine and were the last to leave the restaurant. The most intimate confessions had poured out of us.

The bottle in front of the candle—the surface of the wine sways like a dark disk hovering over the red-shaded liquid. It's too bad that Julio is so obstinately orthodox.

8

Mother takes the medicine bottle, pours out three pills, and swallows them with the help of a glass of water. She puts her hand to her forehead and lays her head over the back of the easy chair. Within half an hour, she'll calm down and won't go back to telling the same stories over and over. Ever since I got here, she hasn't stopped repeating how Bob left her, their last argument, and the different versions of her life with the young buck. Well, I don't feel like I have the right to tell you that Bob just exploited her. She is still very hurt, and, basically, what she does is play with the truth for her own advantage. She swears to me that Bob never had anyone else, and that their breakup was due to Bob's personal need to get a job and to affirm himself socially, rather than a real cooling off between the two of them. Mother was blessed from the crib with the ability to block out the sun with a strainer. While married to Father, she acted like a *grande dame,* as if we still lived in the golden years of the company. The truth is that her family, although not having a great fortune, spoiled her. She insisted on holding weekly receptions with pomp and circumstance, and on maintaining a circle of friends that Father, with all his bonhomie, considered—just between you and me, my daughter—to be tremendously maddening.

With her feet on the footstool wrapped in her light silk flowered peignoir, she caresses the Pekinese, which always sniffs at me. She would've fallen asleep now if it weren't for the telephone jangling her out of her rest; she must be thinking it is Bob. It is a friend of hers, and I tell her that Mom is taking a nap after lunch. The Pekinese escapes from her arms and barks at me as I adjust the cover over Mom, now stretched out asleep on the chaise lounge.

9

Yesterday, I brought Marcelo's friend home. We started out on the sofa and ended up in our bed, Heloisa's and mine.

I woke up today with Jucineia sweeping the carpet in the living room. The boy was still sleeping, but I woke him up. He had beautiful eyes, red from sleep, and I told him that he had to leave out of sight of the maid. I opened the door and looked through the slit: Jucineia was in the kitchen. I went there, ordered coffee with two slices of toast, and talked with her while holding the door shut behind me. The boy cleverly slipped out.

I gathered up the sheets and stuffed them in the dirty clothes.

10

The morning comes to consciousness/Of faint stale smells of beer...I remember Eliot's words just as I awaken on the sofa at the ambassadress' house. The sharp light cuts into my eyes like a cold blade. With some effort, I turn over under the covers, swallowed up in the late ambassador's long pajamas. The beam of sunlight marches slowly across the stone floor. Little by little, I awaken, penetrating the world of the living, leaving flashes of dreams, meaningless figures and scenes, and remaining bits of the night before in a secret compartment of my subconscious.

The strip of light has widened and now forms a fan on the ground. I turn over again on the red and cream striped sofa. I have a bitter taste in my mouth; my tongue feels rough. I throw my face between my hands, feeling as if some kind of storm has picked me up and relegated me to this unknown beach. I feel halfway like a clown wearing these loose pajamas of the dead ambassador. What did I come here to do? How did everything begin? The light projects shadows onto the Greek bust on the glass table.

The doorbell rings, and the black houseman goes to answer. It's Hildo Leão, who has come to pick me up. *The morning comes to consciousness*. He wants to take me to the club, so I can take a dip in the pool, cool off, and wash away my hangover. "What shit, guy (again)!"

Renato had called me at noon to invite me to have a beer with him at Fritz's. The conversation had gone on until late afternoon. The sun reddened against the scrub brush; the lights of the bar came on, and night was falling. For hours, I kept my mouth locked shut in front of Renato, in spite of my feeling that there was a lump in my throat caused by that primitive feeling of suspicion that I can never hold back. I looked at his eyes, a deep black, his small hands, his slender fingers holding his cigarette, the glass of beer, his mouth telling me of several affairs with boys, while I was nourishing my jealously, my tortured jealousy, which had started at Luciano's party. That room was so dark. Luciano was playing the guitar with a friend, several unknowns around him listening, moments of silences, murmurings, an instant of laughter let loose, Renato at my side smoking, continually smoking, and his glances crossing those of Luciano. I saw them. I'm certain that I saw them. I caught the two of them looking at each other—Luciano, as if he were playing only for Renato, who seemed to be exalted by the music. My jealously grinds and squeezes and crushes, increasing, as my imagination runs wild, and the torture of being there watching like an idiot as those two are drinking in front of me, adoring each other, taking delight, while I am dressed like a clown, a clown forgotten and thrown into a corner, onto a darkened curtain in the background.

Hildo appears at Fritz's at night, around seven o'clock. I wave to him—oh, great figure—and he comes and sits with us. Hildo has been upset lately with Renato for some little thing that I don't remember anymore, but nevertheless, he joined us and asked for a beer. We talked and talked until Renato invited us to his mother's house on the lake. Heloisa is in Rio, and he had nothing at home to offer us.

Renato's father had been a diplomat in Venice. Sometimes he tells me about his memories of other countries, of cities he has visited, Barcelona, Munich, London, Buenos Aires, far-off lands that I have never visited, nor will never visit. I start imagining, and my childhood brings me only the waves of the sea, the beach, the hills, the city of Rio de Janeiro. Now, I'm isolated in the capital, expelled by the voracity of times from the megalopolis that spews out its sons, swollen, pregnant, decayed, and unable to sustain any more slaves to hold up its pillars.

Renato remembers his adolescence with nostalgia, but he did not want to follow in his father's career. That gypsy life without roots no longer attracts him.

"Ah, no, Europe…you need to see…When I hear Bach, the Bach record that you gave me as a present, I think of a little church in Bonn that my mother would take me to, where Mass was celebrated with an organ and a choir. It's really something. The English governess would go along with us. How I hated that woman, the English governess…"

Leonor appears in the living room. The three of us make an effort not to appear drunk, although no one is really able to stay straight up, even while seated, nor hide that moist brilliance in our eyes that denounces the high alcohol content of our blood. Renato asks his mother for a whiskey, as if raising his finger to a waiter. She replies dryly, and he answers back. The two get into an argument. Then we witness that unpleasant scene where the hosts begin to fight. Hildo and I sink into our shirts like two turtles. Finally, Leonor leaves and, surprisingly, the houseman appears with a bottle of Ballantine's on a tray. We dive headfirst into the "water of life."

11

To seduce him, I'm going to play the part of a fox. With his timid appearance and his blushing over anything, he hides his peacock tail under his black raven legs. Just as in the fable, I'm going to sing of his immense literary talent. I've taken his poems, his stories, his pieces of prose, and, just as with Heloisa, I'll try to give him my full attention—all eyes and ears. Who knows, but I may finally attract him and leave him imprisoned to my will?

I was introduced to him by Grilo before we went out to a little party at the Congress Club. Julio drank, and then pulled off that mask of his as a shy little boy, a reserved intellectual, to show his face of a Harlequin, or maybe of a joyful Pierrot.[43] Well, that's how I came to know the secret. Julio always knew about the friendship between Dad and the rector, who, in turn, would not care to hear of the similarity of one of his teachers to a Greek pedagogue, even though I should never lend myself to the sordid role of the intriguer, much less that of a blackmailer. But Julio doesn't know about that and is afraid of my indiscretion, and he tries to fool me. I take advantage of that and take him as my company for my evenings and weekends with Heloisa.

One time, I wanted to have sex with him. We had stopped over at Renato's house after having lunch at Fritz's. Heloisa was in Rio, and our host promptly fell asleep. I climbed on top of Julio and almost summoned him to screw me. He rejected me. Since that day, I have come to realize that with him, seduction has to be approached very slowly, subtly, without haste or anxiety. Just like with Heloisa. Anyway, I see that the two converge at a common point: the fragility of a bird.

---

[43] Harlequin and Pierrot: traditional figures of Brazilian Carnival and stock figures of the Italian Commedia del'Arte.

12

When I return from Rio, I normally come back with two contradictory feelings: one, that time has not gone by, that I had never really left there, that the time spent in the capital is nothing but a lapse, a dream, a brief, unimportant moment; and two, that on the other hand, I am a foreigner in my own city, since my friends are so different and lead a kind of life so different from my own that their daily problems seem distant and unintelligible.

The city remains the same. Avenida Brasil is still dangerous and dirty; only the billboards and graffiti have changed. The lagoon[44] is still surrounded by more and taller buildings, but there it is, with its mute language of silent, dark waters. Ipanema beach and its coconut trees, and Leblon with its dirty ocean, Veloso, Etoile, Smuggler, the street urchins, the shoeshine boys, the kites, the parrots, the Gloria clock, the pigeons, Colombo, everything. The Monroe Palace is gone, that is true, as well as the Cinema Pax and the Miramar, but the climate is the same. Seagulls glide over that eternal blue that reminds me of the cover of a book of poems by Schmidt.[45] When I am in Rio, I don't remember Brasilia or even the Renato who lives there; only the young Renato who would come all dressed up to pick me up for a ride in his car through the Barra da Tijuca on Sunday afternoons. In fact, it is at a motel in Barra that it happened for the first time between us. It wasn't complete; it wasn't as beautiful as I was expecting. It was horrible. But it was the beginning of an unforgettable period in our

---

[44] The lagoon: the Lagoa Rodrigo de Freitas, located in the southern part of Rio de Janeiro, is a beautiful small body of water that serves for all sorts of recreational activities, including the park area around it.

[45] Augusto Frederico Schmidt (1906–1965): an important poet of the Brazilian Modernist movement. He later becoming a publisher.

lives. (Why do I start to think about Renato when I don't want to think about him anymore?)

When I met with Solange, I felt such a great distance between us, as if I were talking with a stranger. She told me about her husband, her children, her work. I wanted to confess to her about the crisis with Renato, but I held back. Solange wouldn't stop talking, and her problems seemed trifling, lacking seriousness. It bothered me when she mentioned her children and details about each one. Yes, maybe because Renato hasn't wanted children so far and won't tell me why.

Solange had been my best friend since our first years at Sacred Heart. We were inseparable. We slept at each other's house. We had our first boyfriends at the same time, and now…this estrangement, this difference of worlds…. With other friends, the same thing happens, and when Angela, after talking for hours and hours about her separation, asks me how Renato is and how the two of us are getting along, I answer, "Fine, just fine."

13

I went to talk with the senator this afternoon. Carla made an appointment for me. He had red eyes that he rubbed from time to time. He seemed tired and asked me short, objective questions. The interview lasted fifteen minutes.

On the way back, a rainstorm soaked my black suit and my shoes. I had to jump over puddles and puddles to reach the car. I just hope that after all this anxiety, I will get the famous directorship position in the ministry that I so hope for.

14

Grilo Falante tells me:

"For me, you end up with a sort of internationalism that doesn't go anywhere."

We were discussing literature. Fabinho was there, too. Both of them were defending the most nationalist strain of Modernism. At the height of the discussion, I said that Oswald de Andrade was a mere figurehead of the movement of 1922. I suggested that on the other hand, Mario de Andrade[46] really knew his art; he was a respectable name, an erudite person, and a great literary critic, although as a poet, he may not have been all that great. Well, that is how I demolished two icons of our cultural mythology. They spit fire on me like two angry salamanders.

Fabinho, as a good intellectual, if only he didn't wear a beard, did smoke a cigar. He offered it to Grilo, who smoked it, blowing indignant puffs into the air. I was defending the poetry of Cassiano Ricardo, Schmidt, Cecília Meireles, and Murilo Mendes.[47] The two were died-in-the-wool Andrade fans. The recruit, Grilo's current liaison, served as wine steward, keeping us supplied with deep red wine. It was cold that evening, and a fine rain was falling. The cigar went from Fabinho's mouth to Grilo's and back, going fluk, chuk, fluk, chuk.

---

[46] Oswald de Andrade Souza (1890–1954) and Mário Raúl de Morais Andrade (1892–1945): not related to each other, they were the most important leaders of the Brazilian Modernist movement of 1922. Mário was the primary organizer and the more widely recognized literary figure as a poet, novelist, storyteller, and musicologist. Oswald was known mainly for his poetry.

[47] Cassiano Ricardo (1895–1974), Cecília Meireles (1901–1964), Murilo Mendes (1901–1975): important Brazilian poets of the twentieth century also involved in Modernism.

"Oswald is a buffoon," I replied.

Fabinho mentioned his *King of Candle*[48] and Grilo repeated, *"King of Candle! King of Candle!"*

We ended up reciting *"Pasargada."*[49]

Fabinho left around eleven, feeling rather shaky. I stayed a little longer to hear Grilo give advice to his friend, the two embracing on the sofa.

"You need to do more exercise on those arms...."

---

[48] *King of Candle* or *O Rei da Vela*: a three-act play by Oswald de Andrade that debuted in 1937 in São Paulo. A film version in English, *King of Candle*, appeared in 1983.

[49] *Pasárgada*: a reference to the iconic poem "Vou-me embora pra Pasárgada" ("I'm going off to Pasargada"), written by Manuel Bandeira in the 1920s; it describes an imaginary utopia (named after an ancient Persian city) and man's search for it. It has been set to music several times and can even be heard and seen on YouTube.

15

We went out to dinner together last night at the Français, that is, just one night after her return from Rio. She and Renato had fought over some stupid thing, so he fortunately did not come along. He packed his bags and went to sleep at "Mama's" house on the lake.

Heloisa—I don't know if it was nostalgia—was dressed up so nicely that I created the fantasy that she had done it just for me. She had good makeup on and was wearing a new dress bought in Ipanema. I ordered rabbit with a mustard sauce, and she wanted *filet à la sauce béarnaise*. A good Chilean wine toasted our reencounter. (What a noble moment it is when the wine is put on the table and slowly poured into the glass!)

Heloisa spun her wedding ring around her finger and told me about her argument with Renato, her mother-in-law Leonor's possessive personality, the time she spent at her mother's side in Rio, that guy Bob (her mother's ex-boyfriend), and Solange and Angela (her friends in Rio). As she talked, I watched her, enjoyed the wine, and drank in her hazel-colored eyes. (Now she wears contact lenses.)

In the meantime, she looked at me differently this time. I am sure of it. She looked deep into my eyes. It was a different look, more sparkling than I had ever seen before. The candle between us, the wine, the coffee, the liqueurs. No, I wasn't dreaming. I just have to be patient, robustly patient.

16

The radio is announcing that the rains will not be stopping in the next few days, and it appears that they may cause some catastrophic damage in surrounding cities. (It seems that near Belo Horizonte, there have already been some mudslides.) Today, there was such a traffic jam on the bridge that I spent almost two hours there, getting to work very late. Guedes glanced at his watch as I entered.

Mother comes in and very nicely brings me a whiskey on a tray, wanting to mess with my head. She won't admit it, but deep inside, she loves it when I fight with Heloisa and come to take refuge at her house on the lake. She put on my favorite record and started to talk about how I might possibly reconcile with my wife. She was acting like the purest of nuns from a convent, dedicated only to providing help, while I know very well her stratagems. She is going to do everything she can to prolong my stay under her old Mother Goose wings.

17

Carla was looking at me strangely. Could it be...? We went out to eat dinner at the Français the other night, and she kept giving me these deep looks. She told me about a great love she has for a married man. She said she couldn't reveal his name, because he holds an important position in the government. By association, she turned the conversation to Renato, saying that her father has set up his appointment to the directorship of the ministry. Let's hope so.

I go home half dizzy from wine and liqueurs. I turn on the TV, light a cigarette, and immediately go to sleep. In the middle of the night, I wake up suddenly. According to Carla, this happens because of the mixture of wine and coffee. I go to the kitchen, drink a glass of water, and wander around the apartment. The rain has stopped. I open the window and breathe in the washed air, the smell of ground that has been satiated, the flooded ground saturated with water. Starting May, it won't receive any more water, and its body will crack open in fissures, the red land and its grass dried out by the sun.

I feel shivers and I miss Renato. We fought over nonsense. Carla understands me. Only she understands me today. I go back to bed, and, when I'm just falling to sleep, hear the sound of the key in the lock. He walks down the hall drunk and lies down next to me, still wearing his clothes and shoes.

"Renato!"

He doesn't hear me and is deep asleep. I caress his hair. I kiss his face. (How hard it is for me to sleep without that presence next to me!)

The next day, he doesn't mention our fight, nor his quick passage through his mother's house. We eat breakfast practically in silence. Jucineia listens to the radio turned up loud.

"So early in the morning, all that news about crimes, murders," complains Renato. "Jucineia, turn the radio down a bit, please?"

I say that I'm going to learn to play tennis. Only then does he raise his green eyes to me. I add that, after all, it is something to do, a sport. I have never played any sport in my life. He agrees, says it's a good idea. He looks down, and then forgets about it as he stirs his coffee.

18

I can't stand it anymore. I know that I am not mistaken, and they are staring at each other. Luciano plays the guitar; Renato is bent over the window with a glass of whiskey in his hand. I don't have any doubt. Since the start of the party, neither one has taken his eyes off the other. My jealousy is almost physical pain. I down my dose of vodka in one swallow.

Hildo Leão confesses to me that he has a poem hidden in his drawer. I pretend that I am dying of curiosity to read it, just to please my friend and to relieve my sensation of abandonment. Hildo smiles behind his thick lenses and answers that he will never show me his poem.

"Why don't you take writing seriously?" I ask while continuing to feign interest, and I hear my voice coming out of me with no enthusiasm.

Fabinho and Carla come back to the room together with a strange look. They must have been sniffing powder. I go up to Carla's ear, and I beg for a little line.

"In just a bit," she says in a slurred voice.

Luciano plays Villa-Lobos.[50] Fabinho puts his small hands to his face and whispers to me: "Shit! What a pain!"

"Play a samba!" someone shouts insistently. Luciano gets upset and stops playing. Pernambuco grabs the guitar and plays a samba. Outside, the rain continues to fall.

Fabinho talks to the girl who has lived with the Indians in the Amazon. She is dressed and behaves like a survivor of the hippie movement. She says that at first, the Indians appeared more distant with her than with others in the group. Strange. Fabinho wants to know

---

[50] Heitor Villa-Lobos (1887–1959): Brazilian composer of classical music and best known for his "Bachianas Brasileiras."

if Marisa has read Da Matta's[51] latest book. Of course, the Indian specialist had read it. I bend my ear to hear their conversation, thus, taking my attention off Renato and Luciano, who are chatting at the window.

"But tell us something about Da Matta's book."

"Yes, Da Matta is great. If you'd like, I'll lend you...."

"No, I'm not going to read it; I just wanted to know what's it's like, so I could talk about it." Fabinho gives his little hyena laugh.

Hildo tries to converse; Fabinho's and Marisa's voices drift off and get diluted in the surrounding noise. Pernambuco sings a *frevo*.[52] Hildo says that he went to the movies at the English Culture Institute to see Antonioni's *The Adventure*. Tonight, they are showing *The Night,* and on Sunday *The Eclipse.*

"It's a trilogy of human incommunicability," Hildo pontificates. He never gives a personal opinion about art; he always repeats what he has read in some newspaper column or book review. Behind these set phrases, he never runs the risk of putting his opinion to the test. Fabinho, on the other hand, plays the part of an intellectual and comes to proffer some of the most outrageous ideas just to sound original: it is a matter of *il faut épater à tout prix,* one must *épater* at any price. Both covet the attention of Sara, the graduate student. She is dancing with fat Gastão. The couple swings around the dance floor.

I am torn apart. No, I can't hide my jealousy, this burning jealousy that enrages me and thrashes up. Should I join them at the window, play the intruder, and try to join the conversation? I get up. Carla grabs me to dance, but I resist her. But she insists, and I go with her totally without desire. We are two couples dancing to the implacably northeastern voice of Pernambuco. Carla smiles at me with her round face, her glasses, her dark teeth. She is full of ether, joy, and cocaine. And me, jealousy. She swings to the sound of the samba, while I drag myself about. I think Gastão finally has dared to take some liberty with

---

[51] Roberto Da Matta (1936–): prolific contemporary Brazilian anthropologist. He taught in the U.S. at the University of Notre Dame.

[52] *Frevo*: a carnival dance or song typical of Pernambuco, a northeastern state and the character's nickname.

Sarita, who pushed him away and went to sit down by Hildo, furious. Hildo is purring with contentment, and Fabinho is sniffing in a huff. .

Grilo is leaning against the edge of the window opposite the "lovely couple." His boyfriend, even further away, was getting bored at his side. They both had on faces like people at a wake.

"Shall we go? This is crappy," he invites me, after I manage to escape from Carla's grasp.

"Like Dom Pedro, I shall remain."[53]

"When you get together with these shitheads, you never want to leave. I don't understand it. Let's go, Waldir."

Where is Heloisa? There are not so many people here that I shouldn't be able to find her. I feel like doing some mischief with her. I'll insinuate that Renato and Luciano…Look, that's not very hard, and, as jealous as she is…Where is Heloisa? In the kitchen, talking to two women who dress with awful taste and whose names I always forget. I serve myself another vodka. I hug Helo in a show of affection. No, I don't have courage to insinuate anything to her.

"What's the matter, Julio?"

"Nothing at all."

How did Renato go and do something like this to me? "You keep on getting involved with those shitheads, those hypocritical queers, and this is what happens." That's what Grilo would say if tomorrow I told him about my jealousy and the growing intimacy between Renato and Luciano. Why always this feeling of being apart from the others, from the rest of the world? No, Julinho, not self-complacence now, for the love of God. I fall into a tunnel at an attraction at the Piraquê Amusement Park. I'm at the end-of-the-year charity fair. I walk among the booths with my cousin Claudio. He wins a beautiful toy cart in the fishing booth. I covet a porcelain statue of Saint George. I adore the holy warrior; my father told me that he had been a cavalier in the Crusades, like Richard the Lionhearted. For me, he is a prince in sword-and-cape movies. I lose. A little black girl wins the statue with a

---

[53] Reference to Dom Pedro I, the young Portuguese prince and governor of Brazil, who, when the country declared its independence in 1822, stated his desire to stay on as emperor instead of returning to Portugal, thus, taking the side of the revolutionaries.

big smile and says it is her favorite saint. We keep going, Claudio and I, through the fair. Night falls and fireworks blast in the sky.

"Look at Laura," Claudio says to me, pointing her out.

Laura, my cousin, a swimmer at the club, is going around with that idiot, a record holder in the crawl. They are holding hands.

"They are going together."

Claudio didn't need to supplement that scene with his unpleasant comment.

I leave the party without saying good-bye. I get in my car and drive around the Axis. I drive without destination to placate my anguish. I drive and drive, and the city seems to be deserted. All its inhabitants have left, and only I continue on in this desert. I think about going to the Taguatinga to bury myself in that boys' sauna, to fall in the arms of one of them, to forget about the night. No, that would be worse, I know, and how well do I know. I drive on through the desolate city.

19

Heloisa really got it into her head that she wanted to learn to play tennis, to escape her boredom, evidently, and all the frustrations that her husband brings her. That night at their house was horrible, although deep inside I had watched that scene from a box seat. Renato decided to dance with that flirt Sara, and then it began. The two stuck together, talking until almost the end of the party. Heloisa—never very vigilant, with her head in the clouds—began to feel jealous. While we were talking, she never stopped peering/glancing at Renato and Sara on the sofa in the corner, until she got up. I asked, "Where are you going?" as I held her by the arm, but she broke free and called her husband. They went inside. The little flirt looked stupefied. I felt like going there and striking up a conversation just to see where she was coming from, as curious as I was. However, as soon as she discovered that she was alone, she joined her court that included Gastão, Hildo, and Fabinho. It was funny to see the three of them squeeze together on the sofa to make room for their beloved. Who will win her hand, who? I don't think any of them will, but rather Renato, who comes back to the room looking annoyed, put out at life itself. It must have been an ugly fight, I suppose. Heloisa returns. Her eyes are red, so she must have had a crying fit. Okay, this is the moment for me to take her little hand and whisper sweet words into her ear. She needs to understand that a man's love is worthless, that they are all bigamists, trigamists, unsatisfied traitors. Between women, there exists genuine faithfulness—one of these days, I'm going to tell her this explicitly, but today I'm only going to suggest it.

"Did you see? I can't stand that woman."

"That's just how Renato is. He can't bear to see anyone up for grabs."

"No one. Yes, you are right, no one at all. I don't doubt that he screws around, and you know who with?"

"With Jucineia?"

"No! Just imagine. I've heard insistent phone calls from boys. I think he likes boys, too."

"That's not possible."

Heloisa made a face and went back to crying. Tears poured out of her velvet eyes.

"What an ugly thing," she let loose, looking away from me and sheltering herself in her own arms.

"You're not watching closely enough. You know something? I think it's time to find out whether you should continue to live with him or not. It's zero hour!"

We say good-bye down at the doorway. I have made Heloisa see that she can count on me for whatever she wants. The important thing is for her to have complete confidence in me.

20

No. It's impossible to believe. I feel like I'm getting up at the cost of a monstrous nightmare. I am wounded and defenseless. The scandal broke out. I don't know whether to hide, to flee, or face up to the monsters with my head held high. No. I'm sinking in embarrassment, despair, and fear. I'm corralled in a dark tunnel and can only hear the steps of my hunters, shots, and the barking of the dogs that are running to catch me.

My name was in the papers. I went immediately to speak with the senator. He's in Rio, but he must have heard. I called Carla, and her voice sounded very cold. Why has everyone abandoned me at a time like this? I can't look at my wife or my mother, so I rented a little room in this shitty hotel, and here I am, enduring my pain (which has even become physical because I'm feeling cramps), lying face down on the bed, and watching the night fall. Rain is falling hard outside, covering the city in fog. Dams have given way near Belo Horizonte, the radio says, flooding it, covering it in mud, weakening the foundations of its buildings, submerging it. Thus, everything will get eaten away, and I'll be free, free of my disaster.

(I don't know how long I'll stay here. If I get hungry, I'll go out, and then return to bury myself again in this burrow.)

I slept for an hour, and when I cover my eyes, I see the night and I hear the rain. Cars are honking in a traffic jam on W-3 North. I'm cold and hungry. There's no way. I've got to eat something. I put on my jacket and leave the hotel. I walk down W-3 and go into the first sleazy little bar that I come to. The place stinks. I see sausages buried in grease on a cheap tin tray, along with boiled eggs and flattened cake. I ordered a ham sandwich and a beer. I take a seat, scaring away the flies and killing my hunger. A drunken laborer from the Northeast mumbles words at the back over his booze. Two workmen talk at the counter, drinking Brahma beer. A radio plays country music, and that picture of Saint George and the dragon makes me remember for sure that I'm in the backlands.

I pay my bill and return to the hotel. Anguish tightens my chest, and the cramps return. I double up in pain in the bed. Why did all this happen? Why? I open the newspaper on the floor in front of me once again. I reread the article two, three times, without being able to believe what the printed words say.

It was that night. I don't know why I was feeling that way, as if possessed by some kind of devil. At the party, I came on to Luciano and Sarita. I think all my flings with boys and girls lately have left me with a super inflated ego. I must think I'm some kind of James Dean or some other similar stud. Luciano responded to my looks, and Sarita did, too. I gave her a kiss when I took her to the door. Heloisa had an attack of jealousy and wouldn't let me into the bedroom. "Oh, yeah?" I said and I went out like a crazy man.

I drove directly to the Aquarius business district, and, at the traffic light, she approached the car. I had left the door unlocked, and she entered suddenly. She was black and wore a copper-colored wig. I took her to the park. There she sucked my dick. My greatest curiosity, though, was to see a transvestite naked. Completely naked. I asked her to take her clothes off. She refused. I insisted. That's when I saw her face wrinkle in anger, then let go with a brutal laugh in the midst of the silence of that deserted park. Then she pulled out a knife from I don't know where and put the blade to my neck. Her face was a scary mask, and that hair bounced as she shouted for my money. If I tried to push her, the knife would cut my vein, which would certainly happen. I told her I didn't have anything with me, that I had left a party at my house. Her face took on more hatred, her eyes looked injected, and she pressed the knife harder against my neck. Death was staring me in the face. I remembered that I had only my checkbook with me. The transvestite ordered me to fill one out quickly. My hand shook. I had never been attacked before, and the guy looked very strong. I made out a check for Cr$ 100,000.[54] She dug the tip of the blade into my neck and ordered me to drive back downtown.

When I left her at the bus station, I went into panic. My legs could hardly push down the clutch. I was pretty sober for a drunk man. Parked in the lot, I could hear the scraping of the windshield wiper. That's when I made the worst decision of my life. Instead of forgetting about the hundred thousand, I went to the police station to file a complaint.

The scene at the police could not have been more like something from Dante's *Inferno*. A prostitute beaten up, covered in purple blotches, had just come in shouting, and the night officer was hitting his fist on his desk. Everyone was shouting as if in a state of war. I walked up and told my story. A reporter appeared and took everything down, too. The officer smiled.

"I think it's a tough one, but we'll see what we can do."

The reporter came after me and pushed me for more details. I turned my back on him and went home, still hearing the shouts of the beaten woman.

I slept in my office. The next day at work, the secretary came and showed me the newspaper. She was pale in shock—everything was there in detail. What the shit! I'm totally fucked. I ran from the room and spotted Guedes's look; he was peering in the filing cabinet. I fled; I simply fled. Soon, the whole ministry would read news that described an assault by the transvestite. *Punishment, punishment,* I thought, as I crossed the hallway and escaped down the stairs— punishment for having followed my instincts. Mea culpa, mea culpa. The boys, the sister of my friend Luciano, Sara, the transvestite. And Heloisa, who didn't deserve any of this.

I can still see the enormous black face of the transvestite laughing at me, his eyes wide open, sparkling with hatred, and the cold blade against my neck. In the newspaper, the report read: "Mr. Renato Araújo, an important official in the such-and-such ministry, was the

---

[54] *Cruzeiros*: the currency used in Brazil from 1942 to 1986. At 1970 exchange rates, Renato's check would have been worth about US $25.

victim of an assault yesterday at dawn by the transvestite Mirna, whose real name is…"

I have more cramps. No. Tonight, I'm not going to sleep, I'll just go over this bitter nightmare, this horrible nightmare that still threatens to swallow me up in its whirlwind and drag me to its dark depths.

DROUGHT

1

One more serve. No, I really don't have the least sense of aim. Besides, the racket is heavy, and I can never hold it in the right position, so the ball goes in the wrong direction. It flees from me, and I flee from it, since I am scared to death of getting hit. From the other side of the net, patience, he gives me another serve that I cannot return. The ground of the court looks redder in April, when the rains slow down a lot. The sun burns my bare arms that are shaking from the tension to hit the ball. A dark-skinned boy picks up the balls in the corner of the court; he is now sitting on a bench, shaking his skinny legs.

Well, the game ends for today. I think that never in my life am I going to learn tennis. I go walking in his direction. He wipes the sweat off his forehead with the back of his hands, and he comes toward me, with the racket held over his shoulder, and bends across the net. The instructor is dark and young, in spite of the two grooves that are already appearing on his face. His hands are thick, his fingers short, his arms hairy. He explains the defects of my playing. His face changes when he laughs, even when he just smiles. His hair is short, dark, and slightly curly.

I'm going to take a dip in the pool, the quiet blue waters, that plastic blue of swimming pools. From the airplane, the pools of Brasilia looks like little aquamarines against the red earth. I cool off, the bubbles glancing across my face. I can't open my eyes underwater, but they say that the sight is lovely. What a great dive, wow! I think I always do a belly-flop. He takes a long time to come to the surface. No, there he is, and he shakes out his hair. He complains about the cold. We talk in the water, in that position of a swimmer where we are halfway seated, as if half the body were in space with no gravity. We talk about tennis, of course, and we hold our arms above or below the water, relaxing from the class. The waters move; a breeze blows the purple bougainvillea.

"No, you'll learn quickly," Inacio consoles me.

I head for home feeling cool, but then I begin to sweat inside my car. Has Renato already gotten up? On Saturday, he lounges in bed until eleven, sometimes until noon. Yesterday, we stayed awake until the last movie was over.

No, he is making his own breakfast, since Jucineia, starting last week, has been taking Saturdays off, too. How times have changed. I remember at home, Benedita had every other Sunday off. I give him a kiss, and he grumbles a good morning and stirs his coffee and milk slowly. I sit down and nibble on the crust of bread.

Renato has been well behaved since that hullabaloo happened.... He got scared, even traumatized. He has been quiet, taciturn. He normally comes home early, watches television, drinks a couple of whiskeys, and goes to sleep. Good-bye late nights out and early-morning arrivals with his suit rumpled and sometimes with his shoes in his hands. In a little while, he is going to read the newspapers, and, around noon, he'll call me to go to the club with him. I don't know if I'm going. I can't stand those women there, especially that Selma, who thinks she's so funny. I used get bothered if he left me at home. Not anymore. I make myself lunch; I read a book; I water the plants; and later, I go to the movies with Carla or Julio, or with both of them. Renato goes to the club religiously. Sometimes I accept his invitations, so as not to appear uncooperative, and then he has been so good lately.

I lie back on the sofa and pick up the newspaper supplement, while Renato reads the first section. I tell him about my progress in tennis class. He smiles without raising his eyes.

Finally, the senator was able to stifle everything, so that a tiny little piece on the police page wasn't going to ruin his career. The senator thought it would be a good thing to wait a bit before doing his transfer. In the meantime, his adversaries have their eyes open and their fingernails sharpened. The little news report spread like a trail of gunpowder inside the ministry. But one must hold on, be patient, as I have told him myself several times. Renato is anxious anyway. He has just acquired tics. Carla has talked with him, and, because Renato respects her intelligence and experience in these matters of power, thanks to her talks with her father, he has calmed down.

I was sorry for him at the time. But I believe his version of the story, not the one they tell at the club. Renato was mugged, and that's all. A mugging can happen to anyone. Now, if it was done by a transvestite, that is a problem. And the rumors…. Now, everyone knows transvestites are armed. Almost all of them are thieves, with a pimp behind them. It's just pure luck that the police were able to catch that Mirna at the door of the bank and even luckier that the bit of news didn't get out. Renato had to go give his deposition, and I wanted to go with him, but he wouldn't let me and told me horrible stories. It seems that the transvestite shouted out sordid details about his supposed relationship that night. (Then, I don't know. I already suspected that Renato had something going with some boys who used to telephone here but…since they never called again, I think that it was nothing more than a fantasy of mine caused by jealousy.) The transvestite was an atrocious vulgarity. He even roared that Renato had passive relations with him. What a horror! Also, one could hardly expect an honest confession from a man like that.

2

"And you believe that story?"

"That's what he told me," I said.

"Yes, he did. But not the transvestite. He told a different story: he said that when they were screwing, Renato was more the woman than he was," Grilo repeated what the newspaper had published. "It's obvious that he's gay. You want to hide it, but the fact is that Renato is a queer. That mugging story doesn't convince me one little bit."

"The stupidity of his going to make a police report. Now—as all lawyers like to say—he started up the machine of justice; the process is not going to stop anywhere. Renato's career at the ministry is finished!" declared Pedro, twisting his cigarette in his fingers.

"I don't think so. I think that the thing has died there," I said.

"He's a big old fag, that Renato. I always suspected as much. Julio swore that he wasn't, but I knew," declared Grilo, with his head bent over one of his hands, his arm supported on the back of the sofa, and smoking like crazy.

"In any case, I cut out the news item and put it away," Aldo revealed with his hissing voice. Everyone was surprised.

"No, it's nothing. But in case of any doubt, it's a guarantee," he explained his gesture. "Everyone knows that Renato's father had a lot of friends in government, and if he is in the position he's in, it's because of his father's good name. Everyone knows that the senator is a close friend of the couple, and that they visit each other's homes. Now, in this country, you can never tell. Things change quickly from one hour to the next at the rhythm of a waltz. If they accuse me of anything someday, I'll just pull out the article with his photograph."

"That's dirty!" I exclaimed.

"Dirty?! If I feel persecuted or unfairly dealt with in the ministry, I won't hesitate for a moment to go to the personnel department and show the little article to them. If Doctor So-and-So, who today is the director of I-don't-know-what, was taken in by a transvestite and caused a huge scandal, how can you accuse me of anything?"

"I think that's paranoia," I answered.

Aldo shook his shoulders, and his eyes took on that sad expression as the orbits moved in several different directions.

There was a certain melancholy about the afternoon in that predusk hour, as the poet Fernando Pessoa would say, with fluffy clouds floating in the April sky.

I never told any of my friends about the night that Renato and I went to Aquarius. Deep inside, I find the story of the transvestite strange, but he swore to me that it was true. In reality, what really happened is of no interest. It was luck that the senator took care of squelching/suppressing/silencing it all. I don't believe that this will hurt him in the long run. Carla would not like to see the strings of the puppet suddenly slip out of her hands.

3

When she told me, I couldn't believe it. All of me ceased moving; a cold wave arose from my stomach; my eyes clouded over. Did I really hear correctly?

We went out to the country place on Saturday. We had eaten *tutu*[55] with fried bacon bits, and now I was in the living room, cutting out pictures from magazines for my collages, drinking my whiskey, while Heloisa was sitting on the bench under the window. She said something about hummingbirds and suddenly came out with this:

"I have taken a lover."

My gestures froze. A silence overtook everything: the house, the yard, the whole place, the two of us. My hands shook. I wanted to say, "What?" But it would be a lie; I had heard perfectly well what she had said, and she would simply repeat it, emitting those sounds like a slingshot. "I have taken a lover." To my torture, but relief of my inevitable curiosity, she continued:

"My tennis instructor, Inacio. We made love. First, he gave me a kiss in the pool. Then we agreed to a rendezvous. We went out one night to eat at the Xadrezinho, do you know it?"

"We've been there before."

I heard scissors cut through a sheet of paper.

"Well, yes. I went to his apartment. Very easy, like a very easy woman, you know?"

Then I didn't say anything. I felt cries stuck in my throat.

"We met a few other times. In class, he always treats me with great affection. I am scared to death that someone will see us on the court

---

[55] *tutu*: a dish consisting of beans thickened with manioc flour (*farinha*) into a sort of paste.

133

when he hugs me or kisses me. After all, everyone knows that I am married."

I remained in a silence that was impossible to break. The news hit me deeply. I put the scissors down on the colorful clippings and got up. Heloisa was still seated at the window without turning her face toward me. She had told the whole story while looking out, as if watching that big tree in the yard. I poured myself another glass of whiskey.

I could say, "I think that's great for you" or "I love you. Do you know that I love you?" But I didn't manage to say anything. Heloisa's words left me speechless. I felt that she was restless; she jumped from the window, went out to the yard, came back, looked through the clippings, and sat down on the sofa.

I sat back in the rocking chair, which rocked me until sleep came, a deep sleep of forgetfulness; let it carry me away.

4

The senator limited himself to telling me—or to having me told through intermediaries—that I should wait for the "thing" to cool down. Well, in Brazil, scandals get forgotten quickly, but in truth, only six months have passed, although I am not such an important person as to remain in the sight glass of my adversaries. That's what you think, Renato. As soon as you are promoted, the buzzards will fall on top of you, infested with envy, and they will remind everyone about your scandal with the transvestite. Holy shit! How did that happen! And to me, fuck! I was going too far, that's true, I was walking on the edge and defying danger. So now, I am awaiting further instructions from the senator.

Heloisa has been excited about her tennis classes, you know, Mother? No, she's gone beyond that nervousness now. We don't even fight anymore. We have invited the greatest peace into our home. She says that someday she wants to play tennis with me, that she's going to give me a whipping. I can't wait to see that.

Heloisa doesn't pester me anymore. She's calm. I think women really just need a distraction, a hobby outside of their work. This way, she can relax and not come home upset over problems at the university, about problems at home, Jucineia, prices going up every day. I know very well that this exists, that I have to become involved in the management of the home, but not as soon as I get back from work. Shit! Heloisa lets loose with a recording of her laments and interminable demands! Then she complains that I lock myself in my room to listen to my music in peace!

The drought is reaching its limit. The humidity went down to sixteen per cent, the radio says, naturally fudging a bit to avoid causing a public calamity.

I started seeking out Alexandre's sister again. She told me that he had moved to Curitiba. He entered a ballet company there. He's got to be dying of jealousy. I can't do anything. I'm already loaded up with boys, and his sister is much more tasty. Once in a while, we go out together. We take car rides around the lake, and later we go screw in some motel. It's good. The two of us enjoy it. She's only nineteen.

Julio never calls me anymore. I think he's mad at me because of Luciano. Fuck him! I have no desire to screw that little prick of a queer.

I got home from work earlier today. Heloisa isn't home. I go into my office. The silence weighs over the deserted interior of the Quad. Sunset tinges the buildings in the same color as the clay on the ground of the city. I pour myself a whiskey. I put the glass down on the desk. I stir the ice while watching the movements of the night, undisturbed by the weight of silence and by the slow burn out of the day.

5

He pulled me by the hand into the bedroom and kissed me. His kiss was intense, as if trying to swallow me up. Then his embrace engulfed me, and I felt submerged in his substance. It was as if he were reducing me to nothingness and putting me at his mercy. If at that moment he were to drag me over an empty abyss, I would let myself go without struggle. His mouth devoured mine and mine devoured his in an unstoppable desire to be swallowed up, each buried in the darkness of the other. Our arms did not know whether they were caressing or tying each other up in a final embrace.

My skin felt the sliding of his slow hand across it and tightened completely, like seaweed that reacts when touched at the bottom of an embankment of rock. And darkness became clarity, a clarity that we barely guessed as we half opened our eyes. Ah, and to see him in the semidarkness of the room, to try to find the mystery in his eyes, or try to pull him deeper into my innards, into my subterranean spaces, into my mysterious depths.

To have him, just that, to have him. Completely. And to caress his body and kiss it, and bite it and lick it like a sacred temple. Lord of my madness.

The struggle begins at the fulcrum of the night. We sweat. He takes me in his hands and manipulates me like an object. And we gallop furiously across the lunar plain. We struggle and we run; beasts loosed upon a white field.

"Inacio," I sigh, and he breathes heavily, until he let go with what is almost a moan of pain.

We are. He and I. Thus it is on the prairies of the night: horses awakened before the appointed hour.

6

To my despair, Luciano enrolled in the monograph course on Jorge de Lima[56] that I decided to give this year. When I read his name on the roll, I froze: and now what? To see him twice a week, hanging on my words, with his eyes on me for an hour and a half. Shit! I have to pretend and protect myself with masks and boots. I will keep my face unreadable during class. I can't give any signs in front of him.

It's been some time since I've spoken with Renato. On the other hand, he doesn't call me either. Heloisa—whom I run into every day at the university—tells me that he has been going around pretty somber since that business with the transvestite. Of course. And to get involved with a transvestite, hell. If he had confessed his lust for a transvestite, I would have warned him. If it weren't for the senator, his career would really be fucked.

Heloisa adjusts her glasses. (I don't know why she doesn't use contacts at the university; it would be so much better...) She confesses to me that she has found a lover. So much the better. Renato hasn't given shit about her lately, and he even got to the point of treating her wretchedly or even flirting with others in front of her, like on that night when Luciano was playing.

Her lover is her tennis coach. Wonderful in bed, she says. But that's all. Inacio doesn't know about anything but tennis. He is hopelessly unaware of cinema, politics, and art in general, let alone literature.

"He's probably never read a book," Heloisa supposes. "Doesn't matter. At least he satisfies me in other ways."

I went to a recital by Luciano the other day. He played Vivaldi's *Concert for Guitar and Orchestra*. The music and Luciano's black

---

[56] Jorge de Lima (1893–1953): renowned Brazilian poet and novelist from the Northeast and known for his Christian mysticism, regionalism, and his "black poetry."

eyes transported me to a delicious world—with coffee, chocolate, and liqueurs.

I went to greet him afterwards. I hoped that when he found me among his admirers, he would widen his eyes in his special way. But he didn't; he simply thanked me and shook my hand. (How soft and warm is his skin!) I returned home restless and melancholy in equal parts. I wrote a poem that begins more or less like this:

7

That imbecile Inacio talked in the car the whole way, praising his hometown, most pointedly when he saw the graffiti on the overpass: *Brasileia desvairada, Hallucinated Brasilia*—a pretentious and visionary allusion to Mario de Andrade's book[57]—and he proclaimed:

"Yes, that's Brasilia: the city of the future! You know that there is a theory that when the world comes to an end, Brasilia is one of the few cities on earth that will be saved?"

"Wonder of the world...I'd rather be fried by radiation," I responded, and he looked at me with that expression a bird has when eyeing a human. He simply cannot conceive the idea of someone not dreaming about inhabiting a Brasilia isolated from the rest of the earth.

"Brasilia is so beautiful..." he sighs as we drive by Congress.

It's a strange afternoon, with an overcast sky and stifling heat. Surely, it's not going to rain; we're still in July, and the first rains fall in September. Suddenly, though, a drop of water hits the windshield.

"It's not possible...raining in July!" Heloisa exclaims at my side.

"Doubter...!"

I still don't know how to take this situation. With her husband, I knew that the marriage was very bumpy, and so I was just waiting for my turn. In that case, Heloisa would confide in me. (And wow! when she tells me about her encounters with Inacio, with the great confidence of a good friend, it is as if I were forced to drink acid.) She would say that she only likes him in bed, given his insufficient IQ score. If nature endowed Inacio with enviable physical features, it subtracted intelligence from him. Not that he is a guy totally uninterested in things

---

[57] Mário de Andrade, *Pauliceia Desvairada (Hallucinated City)*, 1922: a fundamental work in the then new Modernist movement in Brazil.

of the spirit. He saw my pictures and even praised them and confessed that he likes paintings, especially Impressionism and surrealism.

"I'm going to have a painting by Salvador Dali someday."

"God bless you, my son. I hope that you have money for that."

What most irritates me is that Heloisa seconds his stupid opinions, even Heloisa, who has always been so demanding of taste. We stop at the Beirut. It's five o'clock. The bar is very sparsely populated. Inacio says that he is almost a native *Brasiliense*. His parents came here when he was small. He feels like a *Brasiliense* through and through.

"Brasilia was a necessity. Just look how it grew. It is a spatial, futuristic city, because Brazil is the country of the future. With its size, wow! It has to become a power!

"Are you the son of a military man?" I can't help asking.

Heloisa looks at me funny.

"I am sure that Brazil is going to be a great power someday. When they discover oil in the Amazon, here in Goiás, or who knows where, you'll see! There will be no poor begging in the streets! Brazil needs to recognize its place, its role as a Third World country, a mixed-race country, with its own characteristics, its own identity! Brazil needs to recognize its Indians, its mulattoes, and its blacks, and end this attitude of ethnocide!"

"Huh?" said Heloisa.

"Ethnocide: I read about it once at the university, I think it was in Gilberto Freyre."[58]

After answering Heloisa, he froze, with that expression of a shocked rooster who doesn't understand what is going on around him.

"Glauber Rocha,[59] for example, is the only filmmaker who knows how to portray the real Brazil, don't you think? I've seen all his

---

[58] Gilberto Freyre, (1900–1987): U.S.-educated Brazilian intellectual and sociologist, best known for his book *Casa Grande e Senzala (The Masters and the Slaves)* of 1933, a revolutionary and still controversial treatise on the role of slavery and blacks in Brazilian history.

[59] Glauber Rocha (1939–1981): film director, actor, and leftist activist, best known for his film *Deus e o Diabo na Terra do Sol (Black God, White Devil)*, 1964.

movies. And Gabeira?[60] For me, Gabeira is the great head of our generation!"

I abstained from citing idols. I felt, however, that Inacio was looking for an argument. No, I can't stand that guy anymore. I am here only because of Heloisa. My desire is to toss my whole beer in that idiot's face.

"Where are you going?" the two of them ask, and I am surprised at their being surprised.

"To see a movie. I'm going to the Cultura Inglesa.[61] They're showing a series of films about the *nouvelle vague.*"

"Damn, a French film! God save me! You like French movies, Heloisa? I think they're a bore. It's always that slow thing, that thing my father calls introspective-psycho-subjective!"

Next weekend, I'm escaping to São Paulo.

---

[60] Fernando Gabeira (1941–): a writer and—since 1995—a congressman from the state of Rio de Janeiro, and formerly a leftist activist who was allegedly involved in kidnapping a U.S. ambassador (and is therefore ineligible for a U.S. visa). The 1998 American film *Four Days in September* with Alan Arkin depicts the events.

[61] *Cultura Inglesa*: binational centers sponsored by Great Britain present in major Brazilian cities. These centers give English classes, sponsor cultural programs, and show films.

8

Finding the senator is a problem: he's never in Brasilia. Don't even think about reaching him on a weekend. I believe that every Friday, he has his bags packed to take the plane to Rio. I was finally able to talk with him at the airport where we had taken Carla; she is going to São Paulo for four days. Actually, I found out from her that her father was going at around the same time, although this was not the reason why I had offered a ride to Carla, something that I am glad to do.

We talked for just a few minutes, but enough time to clarify a few important points. The senator believes that the ministry is just waiting for the formal promotion date to include my name on the list, which means a wait of just three months.

I think it strange how the two women kissed in such a slow way. They are friends, I know, but I continue to think that the departure is taking too long.

The day before yesterday, I did a crazy thing. I was lonely for "Julieta," and I couldn't hold back my pride, so I called. "She" wasn't in. Now, we have been friends for so long that it's wrong to get upset over stupid things. I went to "her" house. I knocked and knocked. Nothing. Suddenly, a devilish thought hit me: the boy lives on the lower floor, I know. I rang Julio's bell one more time, even knowing that no one would answer, just to pass the time. That's how I weigh on one side of the scale my irresponsible desire, and, on the other side, my friendship for Julio, my reputation, and my marriage. In recent times, the first has contributed much more to the weight of circumstances.

I walk through the hall with my hands in my pockets, as if looking for a piece of paper lost inside them.

I ride the elevator down.

Luciano looks like a scared rabbit in his hole. He smiles and invites me to come it. I have never seen a bigger mess in my life.

Books and records spread around the floor, on the table, on the sofa, everywhere. Glasses and bottles. Cushions. He apologizes, saying that he is rearranging his library, but I believe that this is the usual position of objects here. Well, artists are known not to excel in organization. He invites me to sit and asks me if I'd like something to drink. I say no, and he starts to play his guitar, a strange way to receive someone. But for people like him, there is probably no better means of communication.

Luciano plays a piece by Telemann.

I applaud.

"Now I'm going to play something just for you."

I feel honored and awkward at the same time.

While he plays, his eyes remain fixed on me. I lower mine and raise them again in an act of courage; after all, I enjoy looking at him.

The baroque music carries me away to some unknown cathedral in Leipzig, where the arcades and incense smoke raise me to a level of ecstasy so sublime that for a moment, it makes me forget about my attraction to the boy.

I applaud. He smiles. The music stops, carrying away with it the enchantment of a cherubim. Now I feel like biting his mouth like a cell of honey from a hive and sinking into the mystery of those dark eyes.

No, no, there is nothing more to do here. I'm leaving. Luciano insists that I stay. "I have just come to pay a visit to Julio, and, since he isn't home, I thought I'd stop by and see you," I justify myself. "Have you seen Julio?"

"No," he answers, averting his eyes.

9

The aroma of coffee invades the living room. Inacio is sitting on the rug, leaning against the sofa. I am in front of him in his apartment. He swears that he makes better coffee than I do. Now, the coffee pot is beginning to whistle. Inacio raises his eyes to me. He is wearing Bermuda shorts; his legs are strong, his trunk carved like a sculpture. We have just made love, and then he comes to me with that inevitable question: do I really like him?

An uncomfortable silence falls between us this quiet Saturday afternoon. The coffee is finally ready. I serve Inacio. We drink without exchanging a word. Inacio turns on the record player and puts on a João Gilberto record, the same one that Carlos likes so much. He is also annoyed by our not having anything to talk about. I leave my cup on a little table next to the sofa and go look at a fern hanging at the window. It falls luxuriantly over the wicker basket. I touch the base; it swings slightly. Two yellowed leaves fall off. The basket squeaks.

"No, don't do that," Inacio scolds me, sucking the rest of the sugar from the bottom of his cup with the little spoon.

I turn toward the window with my arms crossed. The sky is so clear that there is only a single little cloud all alone: a puff of cotton lost in the air. Inacio comes up to me and leans on me. I don't move a muscle; I need to show that I am annoyed. He says nothing and moves away.

I suddenly feel pressure in my chest. Inacio is walking slowly around the living room, looking slender in that satisfied-male step of his. It feels like I've got a seed stuck in my throat. Next to Renato, I feel completely alone. I feel myself fatally alone in the world of men.

10

His little black eyes stare at me like a guinea pig hidden in a bush and chewing grass. I constantly lose the thread of what I am saying, and the students help me to get back on track. I asked a girl to copy the poem *Nega Fulô*[62] on the blackboard, so it can be analyzed. I explain Jorge de Lima's nationalist phase; Luciano sniffs and doesn't take his eyes off me. I avoid facing him, but I hear his nasal voice. It's impossible to forget about his presence in the classroom. The class ends. Everyone gets up, and one student remains seated. It seems like he is making an excuse to be alone with me. When I speak, he pays incredible attention. He looks deeply into my eyes. I feel his breath, the air that he has just exhaled. Luciano. The chalk is rough in my fingers.

"Have you ever read Lucio Cardoso?"

"No," he answers.

"Read him, then. You'll like him."

"What do you recommend I start with?"

"The *Crônica*."

He touches my back as a gesture of departure. How I want to throw myself completely at him and hug him furiously! Luciano disappears across the threshold of the door. From afar, I hear his constant sniffing.

Downstairs, I run into that student who asks me for a ride almost every day, since he lives in the Quad next to mine. He seems to wait for me, but he acts like someone who just happens to be leaning against the pillar. His name is Mauricio; he wears glasses, and he's short and thin. Very shy, he almost doesn't talk, which bothers me a

---

[62] *Essa Nega Fulô*: probably Jorge de Lima's most famous poem. It relates the life of a woman's black slave who is taken advantage of by her husband.

little. If he doesn't want to talk, if he is really only interested in getting a ride, okay, let's take our daily trip home in silence.

Grilo calls me up, because Waldir has gone to Paracatu, where his family lives. He invites me to go to the sauna at Taguatinga. I hesitate. Grilo insists. I finally give in and agree to go by his Quad at eight o'clock.

Right at the entrance, there is a poster hung on a plywood divider that shows some interior shots of Finland in the summer. The Northeasterner at the bar recommends that we leave our valuables with him, and he gives us keys to the booths. Some customers are sitting at the tables of what looks like a roadside restaurant. The booths are located in an adjoining room. After we take off our clothes, Grilo and I go down to the sauna itself. There is no one else down there. We walk into the steam.

"This here is a terrible today. It has no future," Grilo predicts, rubbing his nose in that allergic tic, while huddling in a corner. I can see only his silhouette in the clouds of steam.

The shower is awful. From the head, just a weak stream of cold water trickles out. I shiver all over, so I lie down on a lounge chair. I look at my body and see that I am a bit fat. Since no one comes down, we go up to the bar, if it can really be called that.

The boys are beginning to arrive. I can't tell who comes first, or if they come in together, but they simply walk in, sit at the tables, go to the booths, or stand around, talking to each other in groups. It's like a happy hour. I see a dark-skinned boy talking with a guy in his forties. I mention to Grilo that the older guy looks like a congressman. I go to the counter to pick up another bottle of beer for me and Grilo, who seems rather withdrawn today.

I stare at the boy. He recognizes my look. When Grilo goes down to the sauna, naturally following another promising sign, the boy comes over to me. He sits facing me at the table.

"I'm looking for a job, and that guy there, a friend of mine, said he'd find me one," he tells me. "Do you play any sport, dude?" He tries to make conversation.

We descend into Hades. We enter the Turkish bath. There are other people there now; I can see silhouettes, including Grilo's. A tense silence reigns in the cubicle, a silence like that in a dentist's waiting room or an elevator. I don't allow myself to get upset. Two beers were quite enough to reduce my fear and my shyness. After all, isn't it why we are here? I rub the brown, hairy thigh of the boy who plays sports. He doesn't move. We go out, take that thin cold shower, and go to lie down on a lounge chair.

"Don't you want to get a booth?" he proposes and shakes his curly, wet hair.

We enter a booth. I lock the door and turn out the light. We lie on our towels on the cushioned floor. Little by little, his body takes on a shape, like on a photograph being developed, from the depths of darkness. I approach him. Here I have that Greek statue in my possession, as if abandoned in the basement of a temple. I grope him, feel his contours, his hills and valleys: I memorize them.

We exit the booth and go up to the dressing room.

"Hey, man, how about helping me out with a little dough? I've got a date with my girlfriend tonight, you know?"

I go out to the bar and make a withdrawal from my wallet, about five thousand *cruzeiros*,[63] that I hand to the slut in the dressing room.

I meet up with Grilo on the stairway.

"And so? How was it? Did it work out?"

"What do you mean, Grilo? Don't be vulgar. I fucked the congressman's guy. And you?"

"Crappy—I thought he was a hustler. I grabbed for his business in the steam and guess what? He was big old woman, more woman than I! Let's get outa here!"

"So soon?! I'm just beginning to have fun…"

"Whore! Whore! You really are a fucking old hen. Okay, then, let's stay, but just for one hour, huh? I don't even want to think about greeting the dawn in this place!"

"Hour and a half?"

"One hour! Come on, buy me a beer."

We drink another beer and, suddenly, Aparicio Gama appears, with his enormous Gloria Swanson eyes. He begins to sing of his

---

[63] Cr$ 5,000: about one U.S. dollar at the 1970 exchange rate.

interminable passion for a workmate, a little shriveled up bureaucrat with no charm whom, as a code, Aparicio decided to call by the prosaic nickname of Lourdes Magalhães. I really can't take any more of his stories. They don't hang together. Aparicio unilaterally falls in love, and now he is beginning to weave fables and suppositions, trying to convince us, and himself, naturally, that the guy harbors repressed love for him. Grilo yawns. I cover my mouth with my hands. Aparicio changes the subject and tells us about a musical he saw in Rio last weekend. He imitates the main character with all his grimaces and makes it clear that he knows all the songs by heart. He lives in his own world of masks, illusions, and stage lights. He is a displaced artist, a strange figure stuck in the audience, who wants to be on the other side, the side with the reflectors and the action, since he believes that is really his place and not here among gray, apathetic bureaucrats.

I go back down to hell. A group of boys challenges each other by lifting, each one in turn, a barbell weighing about seventy pounds. My eye catches one of the younger ones in particular. Aparicio and Grilo come down. A blondish boy tries to make conversation with Aparicio. The baby of the group comes to sit next to me on a lounger. We talk. The boy says his name is Jaci. Like the moon. Like the moon of the Tupi Indians.

"Let's go to a booth."

He looks at me with his inviting black eyes.

"You won't be sorry."

And I really wasn't sorry. The boy is a fury in bed. We spent hours in the booth.

I look at the body that a few minutes before was lifting the very heavy barbell. Jaci is short but has a beautiful face. He asks me for a ride back to the city.

"Be careful. There's a doctor after that guy. It seems that he took him to his house, and some things disappeared. But I don't know, a ride's okay, just don't take him home," the Northeasterner at the bar warned.

I can't find either Aparicio or Grilo. Shit. I'm leaving anyway. Aparicio has a car and can take Grilo. I'll take Jaci, the dangerous boy.

I don't have anything against hustlers. Don't guys go for prostitutes, too? And doesn't phallocratic society justify prostitution by calling it cynically the "oldest profession in the world"? I haven't found any partners in months. I can't find anyone I like in the nightclub or at the bus station. Look, my sexual impulses torture me, and I can't keep from looking at the hustlers at the Taguatinga sauna. I've been afraid of soldiers lately. There were two murders and a robbery a short time back, and a friend of mine was mugged and tied naked to a tree in the woods some kilometers from the Pilot Plan.[64] No, there's nothing else I can do. Luciano doesn't love me; he doesn't even respond to my supplicating stares burning with passion. To tell the truth, I don't even know if I'd want to make love to him. I think of him as such a spotless, pure character…Maybe I'd prefer to love him like this, from a distance. Everything is so impossible…that boy is a student of mine, to get something going with him. The Axis is in front of me, night having fallen over the capital. The car swallows up the road. Jaci, at my side, doesn't say anything. He insists on answering "just so" when he wants to confirm some question of mine.

"Are you staying at the National Hotel?"

"Just so."

He doesn't talk, only looking like a bewildered child; the Axis flies beneath the car. I take his small hand.

"Did you like spending the afternoon with me?"

"Just so."

---

[64] Pilot Plan: *Plano Piloto*, the original layout of Brasilia in the shape of an airplane—the central part of the city.

11

I spent a terrible afternoon grinding my teeth from jealousy, trying to draw until the telephone rang. Heloisa. She had broken up with Inacio. A tremendous relief like I had never felt before, as if my hands had been relieved of two briefcases full of lead tied to my wrists with chains. "Hello?" she said from the other end of the line while I was as silent as a cretin, with no voice vibrating in my throat.

"Hello, hello. I'm listening. I have the hiccups. And you? Are you okay?" I managed to articulate. Heloisa said she was going to come by. Since I don't have any champagne, I put a bottle of white wine in the freezer. Oh, it's not possible but finally! Finally, she has broken free from that jackass.

I drop onto the sofa, run my fingers through my hair, light a cigarette.

I came home from São Paulo Sunday night, hoping to find a note, get a phone call, but there was nothing. Until Friday, nothing. Today, I got up at eight—something that I used to do only when I had analysis on Saturday—desperate. There was no use in pretending I was restless. I went shopping just to relax. I ordered a frame for one of my pictures, et cetera, et cetera. These little errands, if they don't build a fort, at least they can build a provisional wall around our fragility. As I washed the dishes, I fell apart. I fell hard, unable to come back together. Yes, precisely what I felt was a disintegration, as if all the parts that make me up were successively dismantling, like those objects that bang together and fall when you can't hold on to them. I held my hands tight against the marble of the sink. It was a sort of vertigo. The water was going around in a whirlpool and was swallowed up by the drain. I breathed deeply, tried to react; I saw a slice of white sky between the slats of the window. Nicolau's voice irritated me. It's no good. I grabbed a whiskey. I put a song on the record player. I felt better. It's almost noon, and the stifling air is still in that peak of draught.

I remove Nicolau's dish of sunflower seeds. I converse a little with him, and he limits himself to saying "son of a bitch, son of a bitch." I put on the record favored by the two of us women in a perfect act of masochism. I remember the weekend in São Paulo with Silvia and Fefê—how good it was to see them again, the dinner at the Mexican restaurant, the visit to the São Paulo Museum of Art, and the lunch at Traineira, the flow of white wine, *poire* and cigars—and then the telephone rings.

"Hello? Hello?"

"Hello, hello, I can hear you. The problem is that I have the hiccups. And you? Are you okay? Was it a final decision?"

"Of course, it was final. I couldn't take him anymore. Great in bed, but such a nincompoop. He was just an inch away from starting to crawl around on all four…"

"He wasn't even that far."

"Are you going to be home? I'm going for lunch with Renato at that shitty club, and then I'll come by your place so we can talk, okay?"

Of course, it was okay. I relaxed. I held my neck with my hands and closed my eyes. Finally, things weren't going so badly. I felt wrung apart with jealously on the plane, imagining the most salacious scenes between Heloisa and Inacio. Even after that heavy lunch, I couldn't doze off. I was masochistically digesting my (almost) nonreciprocal passion.

I think about lunch and call Julio. He answers with a hoarse voice. He tells me that he has a hell of a hangover, and that yesterday he went to the sauna at Taguatinga with Grilo. I have nothing against that. I don't want to be a moralist or anything, but I simply think he doesn't need to behave like an old fairy and pay for boys at the sauna. I don't share my opinion with him. At my invitation to lunch, he says he feels horrible, since he apparently went to a nightclub after the sauna, where he drank that wretched counterfeit whiskey.

"That's a sure headache," I offer.

He agrees, but doesn't go to lunch with me. Sometimes Julio behaves very strangely. I believe he thinks that I take time away from him that he could be spending with men. Far from me to do that. I just like to be with him, that's all. Well, I get in my car and head out to the country place. But what if I take too long? If Mom and Dad keep me there too long, and Heloisa comes by here? That's certainly what will happen. No, I'll go have lunch alone at Fritz's. Who knows? Maybe I'll meet up with someone there. Fabinho, Hildo Leão, Gastão Abrantes, all the intelligentsia at the university, from left to right.

12

I asked Luciano to record that rare Quarteto by César Frank for me. Saturday morning, I went out to buy a new tape at the Conjunto Nacional, and then went to his house, in the same Quad as Julio's. We ended up spending the whole afternoon together. It was a little misty, and the heat was stifling. Luciano seemed extremely helpful and interested in showing me his records. He's so cute. To tell the truth, I don't understand much about music, and the little I know I owe to Julio, so I often have to pretend to understand what Luciano is saying. He goes off on tangents about the quality of the recording, harmony, melody, et cetera. I confess that I was beginning to find it a bit boring, but his face is so angelic, so childlike, that I put up with those musical digressions. He tells me that he likes Baroque almost exclusively. Classical music like Berlioz is intolerable to him, and Liszt is impossible.

"You're afraid of emotions."

He seems visibly disturbed.

"Not me."

"Well, I think so. If you reject Romanticism, it's because something in the emotion bothers you. Or maybe it's because you're really very emotional."

Luciano passed his fingers brusquely over the strings of his guitar. I asked him then if he had ever been in love. Luciano pretended not to hear me and showed me his rare records, operas by Handel. I gave up. The tape was recorded, and I asked him to record another of those rarities. Around five o'clock, he opened up a bottle of beer and began to tell me about his life as a student and his prospects. He plans to give music lessons, since there really is no other option for his chosen profession.

We empty two more bottles. The phone rang. It sounded like it's a little girlfriend.

"Are you going out today?" I asked.

"Later on."

Luciano rarely looks at you directly.

Night had come now. Luciano had spread himself out among the cushions on the floor and looked like some divine entity listening to pieces by Telemann. His gaze was directed toward the ceiling. He seemed to be dreaming, navigating among the clouds. It's now or never: I grabbed his shoulder in a gesture that could represent either friendship or attraction. He didn't move. I left my hand on his shoulder; my heart was pounding. I pressed it down and moved it closer to his neck. Luciano looked at me. I was going to say something to explain my gesture, but I didn't: often, silence has greater meaning, more effective, no matter how uncomfortable it may seem. He reacted to my approach and moved slowly toward the window. I pulled my hand back to his shoulder and held his arm. He picked up my hand and kept looking at the ceiling. The record ended, and neither of us moved to change it. This is my chance. I got closer to him and gave him a hug. He simply let himself be led on. I prefer to remain quiet. I cuddled up next to him and kissed his honey-colored hair. I breathed in the odor of his whole body. How people have a particular smell! In the meantime, when I lowered my face to give him a kiss, he got up suddenly and let go of me.

"No!"

"Why?"

"Because."

"Forgive me. Forgive me, I just..."

"I have great affection for you," he said, just like everyone else in these situations. Luciano stood up, turned off the record player, and turned his back to me, looking into the suffocating night. I then felt great embarrassment and tried to explain my attitude—or rather, my attempt at seduction—and I went round and round and gave vacant explanations.

Luciano turned around and came toward me and fell down at my side again. He asked if Heloisa knew about me—that extremely emasculating question. I told him that I had given into my tendencies only a short time ago. He told me that he didn't know about himself; he was confused. He was attracted to girls, but he also felt something strong toward his male friends. Finally, he kissed me. We rolled around among the cushions but didn't go any further. He didn't want to take his clothes off.

I left feeling certain that Luciano would never want to see me again, and I felt like a vanquished devil.

13

It happened. I didn't want to, but it did. I don't know if I really didn't want it to happen. Carla hypnotizes me as a snake does a bird. Maybe it's been just an inconsequential act of mine, a way of provoking jealousy in Renato? Or could it be that I'm really seeking a new kind of love to satisfy this monotony, this vacuous life that I have been leading? The worst thing is that, as I try to justify my actions, I fall into the deepest of doubts.

I always wanted to try out different sensations, sound out hidden universes, and perhaps that is how the occasion arose. I don't want to annoy Carla with my curiosity and senselessness, and that is why I am very clear about how far I could go.

(The smell of her body remains with me when we fall onto the sofa.)

I know that I am crazy, or that a part of me is crazy.

I thought of seeking relief, and I lay down, allowing myself to be protected by her, but what I did lit me up like the trail of a forbidden gesture.

Carla, in the meanwhile, lends her ears to everything that I tell her. She replies. She advises me. We share similar tastes in music, wines, dinners, and car rides around the lake.

I never thought that I would be sorry about a little girl playing around! It is as if the Furies were chasing me now at the end of a tragedy!

I need to talk to someone, to Julio, for example. I pick up the telephone, but he's not home. It's useless—he hardly ever stays home.

There's no other way: I have to calm down. I'm going to drink a whiskey even though I really don't ever touch it.

Okay, it's better now.

Night fell completely. Carla went to the country house to spend the night with her parents and left me alone holding onto this damn weight.

And what if I told Renato what I did? God save me. I think that if he didn't slap me across the face, he would demand a separation.

I remember that in school, there was a girl from a grade above me who would always look at me whenever we crossed in the hallways. At first, I would get red with embarrassment and even avoid her. Then I told Sonia, my best friend, about her. The mother-inspector scolded us:

"You two there, what are you whispering about? Now it is time to study and not talk! The next time I catch you, you're going to the office!"

Sonia had time to whisper to me that the older student looked at her, too, and then she, unlike I, appreciated the flattery.

"Really?"

"Really," she answered with that soft smile of hers.

I then began anxiously to await an encounter with the older girl. When I finally saw her, I raised my head to her, as if in a challenge. She came toward me with her confident step but with her eyes looking at a red-headed friend. A few steps beyond her, our looks met like two blades ready for a clash. She stopped, smiled, and winked at me.

I felt the blood rushing to my face, and I fled to the playground. (Strange, but it's only now that those images are coming to mind.) I saw her again a few times, and once again, I faced her defiant, smiling gaze. Once, she ran her hands along my hair quickly in the maternal gesture of an upperclassman toward a freshman. I was bothered by our physical proximity. What I liked was being courted. I never looked at her again.

Years, many years later, now married, I deliver myself into the arms of Carla, my best friend. Why? What for? To make my husband jealous or out of a long-suppressed desire? If we knew the reasons for all our actions, I think that we would be less troubled souls. However, it appears that in our core, there is a shadow that plots against us, that moves us against our will toward acts never even dreamed of, leaving us confused, unable to understand the reason for the existence of this entity within us.

14

I spent the day grading tests and had to read the stupidest things I'd ever seen in my life, and then I taught two boring classes, which neither my students nor I had the slightest interest in but which had to be taught because of the program. As usual, as I left, I ran into Mauricio under the covered patio, and, as if in tacit agreement, I nodded my head for him to follow me to the car. I never remember where I parked, and I always had to wander back and forth looking for it. Mauricio, who had come with me in the morning (I usually find him at the bus stop "by accident" as I leave the Quad), remembered where it was.

At night, I went to Grilo's house, and, for some reason, the conversation turned to politics. We talked about the Russian Revolution when, suddenly, I was shocked to hear Grilo praising Stalin. What? A tyrant, a bloody dictator!

"Stalin was right. I always admired Stalin. His basic idea was to strengthen the Soviet Union militarily in order to defend itself against capitalist forces, and that's why he didn't measure the consequences."

"He destroyed entire villages and massacred peasants."

"But he needed to preserve the socialism that Lenin had implemented! He wanted to turn Russia into an industrial and military power, and he did! That's what I admire about Stalin!"

"I think he was a dictator like any other, like Hitler."

"Don't be silly, Julio. Hitler was a fanatic murderer of Jews, a crazy nationalist with dreams of taking over the world."

"And Stalin?"

"Not Stalin! He wanted to build up a strong Soviet Union. He said, 'First, let's strengthen Russia, and then we can export socialism.' He wasn't like Trotsky. For me, Trotsky was a nut; he wanted a permanent revolution. He was crazy. Trotsky was crazy!"

Waldir, sitting on the floor with a spacey look on his face, was rolling a joint.

"Well, I still don't see any justification for your Stalin. For me, he was a murderer, a tyrant with a thirst for power. Nothing more, nothing less."

Grilo shrugged his shoulders and looked toward the window, toward Waldir, as if he had decided that I could not be convinced— me, a *petit bourgeois*, as if he were anything else—of the Russian leader's good intentions.

"You can tell right away that you are a person of the right."

"I am not on the right. But even as a leftist, I would not defend authoritarianism!"

"What are you in favor of then?"

"Democracy, full democracy."

"Democracy, democracy. What is democracy? A regime where anything goes, where everything is allowed?"

The argument was beginning to annoy me. Grilo, as always, only seemed to want to show off, to show off his political knowledge and his supposed progressivism. For Grilo, there are no halfways, only blacks and whites, only authoritarianism or confusion, only socialism and capitalism. In order for society to be perfect, it must be tied up, controlled, mutilated. Otherwise, anarchy will rule the world. The multiplicity of human feelings and reactions, everything that belies classification and is difficult to understand, must be abolished, so that man does not escape the control of another more enlightened man: there is no more elitist concept, nothing more *Big Brother is watching you.*

"Waldir's arms are really skinny, don't you think?"

Waldir looked up, checked out his arms, and smiled.

"I don't think so," I answered.

"He should do more exercise. I bought a bar for him, it's mounted on the door, but he is lazy and doesn't do anything all day."

"'He doesn't do anything...'" Waldir complained. "Whadya mean I don't do nothin'?"

"He doesn't do anything. Just look: his arms are like a little girl's."

Waldir passed the joint to me.

"He only knows how to smoke all day. That's what he knows how to do!"

Grilo continued to pester the boy.

"Waldir, get me another whiskey, okay?"

"Ah, shit, Grilo. Fuck! Let me just finish this reefer!"

"Come on, Waldy. Get it for me, will you?"

"Crap."

After the recruit left the room, Grilo whispered to me, "You should do that. Get a recruit and set him up in a place."

"For me, a recruit is just for a one-off. I can't live with a guy like that!"

"Class prejudice."

"Could be, could be, but I don't like it, I don't know, it doesn't sit right with me."

"You go around setting up these impossible loves, then they don't work out, and you come crying on my shoulder!"

"Yeah, well, I need to find someone who is like me, someone I can talk with."

"About what? Proust?"

"Not about Proust, but..."

The recruit came back with the whiskey.

"Want a whiskey, Julio?"

"No, thanks."

"You'll never find what you're looking for," Grilo predicted, putting on a carnival record and dancing around.

"Why do you say something like that?"

"Why not? A queer has to marry a recruit, a dude, and that's all. Right, Waldir?"

15

After Heloisa left, I went out, and everything seemed more loaded with colors: the fields are no longer burnt-looking but golden; the sky is not overcast but bluish-white; the lake is not murky but dark. I hear birds and crickets; I notice red wild flowers opening up in the fields. The music on the radio isn't sad anymore, but rather it makes me feel voluptuous, full of a sweet melancholy that feels good. I am light-hearted and want to preserve this instant for the rest of my life. But I know that it flees from me, as if I tried to catch a butterfly whose wings beat in my hand—either I let it die or I let it escape to its kingdom in the air.

I wanted her to have left something behind at my house, a handkerchief, for example; then I could sleep with it folded over my nose.

16

I fulfill a vital need of mine: to make a conquest. It is as if the object before my eyes were full of an untouchable innocence that challenges me to conquer it. I feel like smashing it with the force of my desire. Then I throw it out like a used package. Maybe this sounds excessively cruel, but I can't keep from behaving this way, and I think that I am going again in the same direction with the boy Luciano. Yes, my will, my near obsession, is to seduce him any way I can, since he almost gave in to me the first time.

I don't know about Heloisa. She is still apathetic as usual, except in recent days when she seems to be inside some sort of a glass cage. At least she doesn't bother me with her stupid insinuations.

Oops!

Suddenly, the telephone rings and interrupts my thought. It was the boy. He said that I had forgotten the tape of the César Frank concert at his apartment. Actually, I had noticed this as I left, but I didn't want to go back and get it, so I wouldn't appear to be coming on to him too strong. I was waiting for his call, but I wasn't really sure he would make it. I had to think fast, and I suggested that he bring it to me, so we could have a couple of whiskeys together. As a student, he probably hadn't drunk real Scotch for a long time. Come tomorrow, Saturday, the day Heloisa always has lunch out with her friend Carla, in the afternoon. What can I do to kill my apprehension until then? I call Julio up and suggest we go to the sauna at the Hotel Nacional, then have a beer around there somewhere. But keep your trap shut, Renato. Keep quiet, very quiet.

17

It's hard for me to write, because one of my arms is immobilized. From where I am sitting, I see a quiet garden and people in white walking around in it. Absolute calm reigns in that place, and I am no longer afraid. Fear of myself. The way I felt yesterday. I never thought that we could be loaded down with a force beyond our will. Finally, little by little, I feel that I am able to string my thoughts together, and, as I remember each step that I took yesterday, maybe I can make sense out of it and find an explanation for what now seems no more than an unordered series of events.

18

It was awful. I don't know how to start. The events get mixed up, and I feel confused. These past few days have been so busy that I can still feel the effects. The worst thing is that I am involved in this imbroglio, both socially and emotionally.

It was awful. Heloisa took a fall. She simply fell, and no one could save her. Well, for some time, she had been held together by the finest thread of emotional balance, until it finally broke. Everyone thought that she knew and simply looked the other way, but it now appears that Heloisa was not prepared for the shock. She loves Renato and did everything she could to hide from reality, to cover up the sun with a strainer. It so happens that with time, the rays not only penetrated the screen, becoming visible to everyone around her, but they heated her up and burned her completely, violently hitting her in the face: it's impossible not to feel the full force.

Heloisa went to open the door to Renato's office just at the moment when the two of them were kissing. He thought she was not home, and he had not locked the door. The light blinded her to the point that she walked unsteadily to the living room, groped the furniture, and went out to the street without saying a word. Renato went running after her, but he couldn't hold her back. She got in the car and started it up quickly.

Desperate, she was sure now about all the rumors flying around involving her husband. She drove without any destination around the Axis until she thought of me. She came by but I wasn't home. Then she went to Carla's house. She didn't want to, because she knew that Carla would be euphoric and take full advantage of the situation. But before she went there, she stopped at a drugstore and asked for two boxes of tranquilizers without a prescription, which she takes. They told her they could only sell her one. She bought one box and didn't go to the Beirut or the Fritz, but to some other bar where it was less likely that she would meet anyone she knew. She ordered a whiskey on the rocks. She swallowed about four pills with the drink and went back to the car. She gave up on going to Carla's house and tried my house again. No luck. I had gone out with Grilo to the sauna at Taguatinga.

The tranquilizers had no effect. She went to another bar, almost outside the city limits, and took more pills, once again mixed with a shot of whiskey. A waiter came up to her, and, noticing her condition, asked if she didn't want a taxi.

"I have my car."

She paid and left the bar erratically. She lay down over the steering wheel. Her head spun, and she felt that she could not go on but turned on the key and started the engine. She stopped at another pharmacy and bought a second box of tranquilizers. She did not want to go to Carla's house but drove toward the southern hotel district instead. Then she went to the Hotel das Américas and called me up in a drunken voice. Carla, in the meantime, was already home. Heloisa paid in advance for a room and took all the pills that were left. But she couldn't sleep; her nervous system was in disarray. Then she thought she was going to die. She tried to call me, but I still wasn't home, so she tried Carla again. She told her friend a strange story: she had been raped in the woods by two black guys who assaulted her in a parking lot, and she was covered in blood. Of course, Carla flew to the Hotel das Américas and gave me a call from there.

"The rape story is pure fantasy, but get over here quickly, because she is a mess and wants to see you."

On the way, I don't know exactly how, but the thing came out of the blue. The thing, I mean, the novel that I have been nurturing for months. I had a sketch of the story, the main plot, but I lacked certain details, certain situations, and certain characters were still not well defined. Suddenly, in the car, the whole plot became clear—I don't know—as if by some interior mechanism geared to soften my apprehension over Heloisa. Well, my first novel was born inside the car, like an unexpected birth.

Oh, I knew this was going to happen someday. One day she was going to discover everything. Renato is so much of a planner...besides being a son of a bitch. He *knew* that I liked Luciano. He knew. But just for the pleasure of a conquest, of seeing his ego satisfied and lifted up. Son of a bitch.

When I arrived, I saw the deplorable scene: Heloisa half awake on the bed, with Carla holding her head. On the radio, a jazz band was playing. She always detested jazz.

"Thank you," Carla mumbled.

Until then she hadn't understood what had happened. We called a doctor. He had her hospitalized immediately. Heloisa was suffering from an attack of acute depression and had taken an overdose of alcohol and sedatives.

The next morning, at the hospital, we were able to find out the whole story. Heloisa knew now that Renato not only cheated on her with other women, but with boys, too, and naturally, she realized that Luciano was not the first. It was as if a bolt of lightning had struck her, and, in a second, she understood Renato's distance from her, his secret outings, his personal crises, and finally the crisis of their marriage. And she fell. She couldn't withstand the force of the lightning. The rumors about him, the suspicions, his coldness and irritation toward her—everything seemed to ferment in the depths of her conscience, without, in the meantime, taking on a precise shape. At the moment of the kissing scene between Renato and Luciano, the picture rose in front of her eyes like a panel of strong colors and brutal figures.

I reproduce the story according to the doctor's report. She didn't want to tell us anything, and since yesterday, she's been in a state of complete apathy.

19

She took two doses of tranquilizers with whiskey while driving like a crazy person without any particular destination. She stopped at a pharmacy, bought one box, and stopped at a bar; she drank a whiskey and swallowed a good number of pills. I think she wanted to crash the car against the first pole. At least everything so indicates. She circled around for another half hour, went to another drugstore, and bought a second box of tranquilizers. She stopped at another bar and drank the same cocktail. I don't know how Heloisa managed to walk from the bar to the car; she's such a weakling for drink. Pain strengthens—sometimes.

After that she made up the story—which I, of course, did not swallow—of the rape in the park. Childishness. Heloisa was so out of it that when she called me from the hotel, she thought I would believe such nonsense. Heloisa is a type of girl from Zion: fragile and polite. Those things can happen to anyone, I know, but that was not what I felt when I heard her torpid voice barely articulating words on the telephone. I saw immediately that it could only have been some big problem, some fight with that son of a bitch. However, when Heloisa showed me her thighs scratched and cut, that shocked me. How could someone get to the point of self-aggression? Then she broke down in tears on my shoulder, and that's when I decided to call Julio. He came running, and we called a doctor who ordered Heloisa's immediate hospitalization.

From home, I called the son of a bitch to give him the news about his wife.

"She is acting like a little victim," was his answer.

I still didn't know the reason for Heloisa's despair, which I certainly was not about to ask him.

At eight in the morning, I was already at the hospital. She had a beaten-down, but calm and even pretty look. I took her by the hand. At first, I realized that she didn't want to talk. Julio came in an hour later, and we talked with the doctor whom she had told what had really happened last night. Heloisa was weak and had an IV in her arm.

The doctor recommended another week in the hospital. Julio and I agreed to alternate nights to be with her. I am afraid that Heloisa will feel very alone and will go back to remembering what she saw in her husband's office.

I liked the nurses. One of them left a message on a napkin on the coffee tray: "You came in very upset yesterday. I hope today you will feel God's holy peace."

Renato got there around eleven looking worried. He kept taking his handkerchief out of his pocket to wipe the sweat from his forehead, and he asked a thousand questions about what had happened to Heloisa, as if I had not already told him about it last night. He picked up her hands and tried to kiss her, but Heloisa rejected him.

"Go away," she said to him.

"My love…"

"Go away," she repeated.

Gracelessly, embarrassed at my presence, Renato ran out the door.

"Do you think I should forgive him?"

"Frankly speaking, no."

20

I went to Carla's house tonight. We talked for long hours. I tried to make her understand that I love Heloisa. In my own way, of course, but I do love her. I admitted my mistake, my machismo, my immoral life. Finally, I did all I could to get across my *mea culpa.* She's the only one who could convince Heloisa to forgive me, to forget everything.

"I never fell in love with any boy or girl, Carla. I am in love with Heloisa, and I only want to live with her, you understand? Only with her. I know very well that recently, well, we've had certain problems, but what couple doesn't, huh? Tell me, what couple doesn't go through crises? Look, this business with boys is one thing…Well, I have thought about going back into analysis. Do you remember when we talked about that? Well, you've been doing it for quite a long time, haven't you? I am thinking seriously about that. You know, I think that everyone has a homosexual side. What has happened to me is that…that tendency has come out, and I always wanted to experience everything that comes into my head, you know? But I don't want…I swear I don't want it. I don't feel anything for boys, that is, no real feeling, you know? It's just—I don't know—a type of desire for variation, you know? But I want to end this. It makes no sense, no reason to be. And this ends up hurting Heloisa. Carla, why do you have that look on your face? Don't you believe me?"

She sighed and didn't answer me. She avoided looking at me. That silence unnerved me. I had to extract some answer from her that very night. I needed to go home with some hope for Heloisa's forgiveness. Carla then issued her verdict: she thinks that we should separate, that our marriage has no future. That's really what she wants; I know very well why. But I cannot give up that easily.

"I'm going to talk with my wife. I'm going to ask for her forgiveness."

"So, try."

The next day, very early, I went running to the hospital. Julio came to meet me at the door and told me that Heloisa had expressly stated that she didn't want to see me.

"Man, quit being a shithead and let me talk with my wife, damn it!"

He blocked the door and threatened to call the staff. Shit!

At the office, to make up for it, I got a great piece of news: I was awarded the hoped-for directorship, just as the senator had promised. And Heloisa is sick right now. Damn!

THE RAINS

1

When I called the hospital, a nurse told me everything: how she had tried to commit suicide and how they had come to save her. Now, she continues to sleep under the effect of strong sedatives. Carla had already been notified and was at her side. I don't know how they decided to call her before anyone else, even before her husband. I had to call Renato myself.

"What? Not that!" was his reaction.

They said that there was no use in going now, since Heloisa was sleeping. He would certainly go later.

According to the nurse, Heloisa had tried to cut her wrists with shards from a broken drinking glass. At the hospital, normally, they try to avoid having cutting objects or anything that could serve as a weapon for possible suicide attempts or with patients in a chronic state of depression. As Heloisa had not been diagnosed as a serious case of self-destructive psychosis, the kitchen was not told to use only plastic cups and bottles.

I spent the night at the hospital, and once she had settled down, she told me everything, never letting go of my hand. She told me how the horrible discovery ("I suspected something, but I didn't want to know until I saw that scene"); about the constant harassment from Carla; about her love for her husband. The tennis player didn't mean anything, only a desire to flee, to free herself from the prison that resulted from Renato's putting her down. ("I didn't even want to make him jealous.")

"So did he get the position to the board?"

"He did."

"Just as he wanted."

I asked if she was going to ask for a separation. Heloisa looked deep into my eyes for the first time since the crisis and told me that she had nobody else: if she were to go back to Rio, who would she live with? With her mother and her boy lover? Never. With her father and Marluce? Never. She didn't have friends in Rio; everyone had changed a lot and was carrying on their middle-class lives. She wrinkled up her face and cried, bent over on top of me. Saved from the dark well of my selfishness and my usual problems, for the first time, I felt sorry for my friend.

"But you can't keep on living with him."

"Did you know about him, Julio?"

Now, I was really stuck. What could I say?

"No."

She set her wet eyes on me, as if she didn't believe.

"You swear?"

"Do I need to swear? You are going to continue not believing me. Renato didn't tell me anything. I think that because we are friends, he was afraid to say anything."

Heloisa lowered her head. Her breathing was quick and shallow. She definitely did not believe me. I insisted then that she had to separate from Renato, since to continue in that marriage would be torturous for both of them. Heloisa answered that I sounded like Carla talking. But she loved him. And that was it. She loved him. And these were the words that she muttered before falling asleep under the effect of the sedatives.

2

The rain was falling like mad outside, and I think: *Oh, my love, why aren't you here cuddling with me, protected from the world in my arms, finally finding relief?*

So, I will paint this picture for you, my love, and I'll use your favorite color: blue. Various tones of blue for you to understand that this picture was made thinking only of you, and a few more strokes of red in that corner, because I want to tell you of my passion that is carefully mixed in and explodes like a streak of fire from an underground volcano—how the volcanoes of Bosch spit out lava to try to reach the sky or imprint their marks on it. A flaming wave that opens like a fan over your skin of sand.

(I think that my attempts at poetry are, at the very least, less awful than the poems written by that son of a bitch.)

Just the act of painting for her fills me with a happy calm.

She is still in the hospital, but she ventured to say that she wanted to go to her husband's promotion party. I did all I could to convince her not to, that she is still recovering, but it was hard. I'm waiting for her phone call now. Just the idea of seeing that SOB makes me sick.

"She put on a long-sleeved dress to hide the bandages on her wrists. Didn't you know that she tried to commit suicide?" I can hear the comments from some of those floozies in the corner.

Idle *candanga*[65] women. Their hair pasted down with spray, earrings, necklaces, heavy makeup, fingernails like the sluts at the Sereia bar. Sluts. They're all sluts.

"But today, it is as cold as in Europe," answers another imbecile.

"European cold? Maybe outside, but here inside, it's as hot as a furnace and I…"

---

[65] Candanga: early resident or builder of Brasilia.

I leave them and look at Heloisa in the middle of the room. The son of a bitch is behind her and is holding her arms—a good, polite husband. They pretend to talk excitedly with another couple. I know the face of the old guy from somewhere. I think he's a friend of Father's or someone who is in the papers a lot. Since I don't really follow politics...I turn over the ice in my whiskey for lack of anything else to do, as if to feign my solidarity within this party. I look for Julio, but he hasn't come yet.

Then an ass kisser comes up to talk to me. It's one of Father's employees. Then another one: it's that guy, Abelardo Carvalhos, with his backward mustache, little round glasses, and curly hair. I sometimes even think he's funny when he tells those stories about traditional Brazilian families, talking about the origin of my name *Rodrigues*, making digressions on the monarchy and the republic and that sort of thing. He seems like a character out of Eça de Queiroz[66] with his theatrical gestures and his projected voice. He just turns me off when he starts to say that I'm the daughter of a senator.

"Your father carries himself like Joaquim Nabuco."[67]

Oh, how that irritates me! And that idiot Lourdinha went to ask who Joaquim Nabuco was. Why? Abelardo launched into a detailed dissertation on the guy's life. As if that weren't enough, he jumped to the royal family and its blood connections with European nobility. What a bore! And I couldn't escape from that little circle? And Julio still isn't here, shit!

---

[66] José Maria de Eça de Queiroz (1845–1900): renowned Portuguese novelist of the realism school.

[67] Joaquim Nabuco (1849–1910): a Brazilian intellectual and statesman. He was a major voice in the abolition of slavery, and, in later life, he promoted the Pan American movement and foreign involvement of Brazil in general.

3

Only Heloisa would arrange to do something like this: slip out casually with Carla to go back to the hospital. Fortunately, not everyone noticed, but even so, there will always be people who will talk about the fact that the two of them left together, wherever they may have been going. Shit! And this can kill my career! My wife, whose obligation is to keep up the home, disappears without even saying good-bye to the most important guests! What will the senator think?

I even heard some murmurings about the bandages on her wrists in spite of her long-sleeve dress. Really, Heloisa…I don't know. I understand that she was depressed, she went through what she went through, but I asked her forgiveness, for heaven's sake! I did what I could to make amends, and she goes and tries to commit suicide! The last straw. Suicide. What for? Yes, because it's obvious that she knew that she was not going to die at all, that everything was just a shitty little drama, and she thought that I was going to come to her crying on my knees in repentance. You were wrong, my girl. You were completely wrong. I have already asked for all the forgiveness that I am going to, and that's it.

The senator asked about the two women. It was awkward; I didn't know what to say. Finally, I said that Heloisa was feeling bad and asked Carla to take her to her house. She would be able to sleep better away from the noise of the party.

"Could it be that she…?" suggested the senator.

"No, no, no," I repeated with doubtful conviction.

When everyone had left, I felt completely abandoned. I fell to the sofa, half sitting and half lying, and looked around at the landscape for an indefinite time: empty and half-empty glasses; full, half-full, and empty bottles; little plates with crumbs of peanuts and leftover pasta. All that gave me a horrible sensation of nausea. The table looked like rubble to me. I felt like vomiting, but sleepiness and alcohol-induced dizziness abolished from my field of vision that pile of objects now transformed into dirty, useless things, along with open, crushed cans, tires, grease, pieces of wood, and shards of glass—in other words, trash.

4

After a week now, I'm feeling better. At least I'm trying. Carla has shown me that life is a struggle, that it is not as easy to live as I had thought. We have to fight every day and fight a lot to rise up and not allow ourselves to be beaten down, because the inclined plane is always there, under our feet, as if challenging us. One moment of weakness, and we roll toward the abyss or wherever. What horror! I never thought that I would fall apart, that I would lose control, me, so sure of myself, so mature, so "cultured," so supposedly strong.

My mother would always say, "Heloisa puts up with pain at the dentist's, pain at the doctor's with courage…That girl never cries, never puts on a scene!"

I always hated to let anyone see me cry. "Men don't cry, men don't cry," my uncles would tell my cousins, and even Renato's father—as he remembers it—used to tell him the same thing since he was little. No, I never saw him cry, not even the time of that scandal with the transvestite. Well, my whole life I tried to be strong, but I don't know why. Maybe it's my temperament. Maybe I didn't want to show my parents that I was weak like them, who were always fighting, or that I was suffering because of them. It doesn't matter—anymore. I suffered what I had to suffer. I cried as I hadn't cried for all these years. I think, finally, it was good, in spite of all the pain.

I was lucky to have Carla at my side. A good friend. And Julio, too. Now, I am living with her temporarily. No, I can't go home and face Renato. I still can't face him. What do I do? I don't know if I still like him. I don't know. At the party, he was so tender with me, so attentive. He served me Coke and hors d'oeuvres, as if he were the lady of the house. He introduced me to all his coworkers, politicians, and important government people. In addition, everything was very well organized; he had hired a *traitteur* to arrange everything. The waiters worked perfectly, and the buffet was worthy of the gods. When Renato wants to, he knows how to organize a good reception. Men do know those things.

The moment I felt his fingers graze against my arms, a long shiver ran through my body. Could it be that I still love him? As soon as she got back from the party, Carla hit me over the head with the idea that I should separate from Renato. That night, I fully agreed with her, but today...No, he had a special interest in showing me off publicly because of his new position. Renato used me, as usual. Besides that, what he did to me...The problem is that a strange force in him undoes any of my attempts to distinguish the monster from the handsome boy.

5

When Renato finished telling me, I froze. I then began to feel an uncontrollable hatred for his whole person, even for the way he drinks beer and chews his peanuts. He wouldn't look at me.

"Wow, you did that?"

"Did what?"

"You knew I liked the boy, shit!"

"I knew."

And he lifted the mug high to drink the last drop.

"I knew, but I didn't think you would take it so seriously. It was just a game."

"A game?"

"Yes, a game. I just wanted to see how far we could go."

I didn't know what to say. What I wanted to do was to get up immediately, pay my share, and run from there, leaving Renato alone at the bar. I had met him through Heloisa, my college classmate in Rio. We took philosophy together. I'm a friend of Heloisa's, therefore, and, in truth, I have nothing to do with this guy. In the beginning, I liked him; I even found him attractive. And then it was obvious that our friendship—or rather, our relationship—became stronger as he began to reveal his tendencies. On the other hand, I feel like an accomplice in Renato's secret life, as if I were betraying my friend. If she knew that I know, she would never forgive me. However, I'd be a bad guy if I were to tell her everything. Something you just don't do—although my desire now is to run home and phone Heloisa and tell her everything that I know. It would be a dagger strike in the back of this son of a bitch who cheated on me mercilessly when he fucked Luciano. And I never thought the boy would be that easy....

So I'm staying put. Renato complains that I am talking to him too little, as if he didn't know why. I turn my shoulder to him. I look into the oh-so-blue sky. I ask about Heloisa on purpose. Annoyed, he answers that she is fine. I suggest we pay the bill, and I am finally free of Renato's company.

I drive idly around Brasilia without the least desire to go home. What will I find there? My sound system, my records, my books, my whiskey: the armored scenario of my loneliness. Grilo is not ideal for these times, but, at any rate, he always has a funny story to tell. He's not the kind of friend you can open up to, never. Don't try to tell him confidential things, because he doesn't want to know, so don't insist. Grilo Falante wants to talk, to be heard, and to hear the laughter and applauses from his eternal stage. I wouldn't need to tell him why I've come, because I have a sullen face. He would immediately try to entertain me, to tell me some off-color story, and thus relieve me of the burden that I'm carrying with me today.

Brasilia looks like an enormous spiral when we are in anguish. A spiral from which there is no escape. How could they construct a city so well adjusted to the private hells of each inhabitant! It's impressive. My anguish increases at its innumerable overpasses and cloverleaves, making it infinitely circular, labyrinthine, leading me to a case of vertigo. And those thunderclaps that announce a rain that doesn't come but threatens to submerge the buildings and monuments and to cover everything in mud, confining us within our homes and cars.

I park in front of the Beirut—empty, melancholic. I don't sit down but return to the car. I go to Carla's house. She isn't home either. Wow! There are times when it seems like all my friends have fled. Brasilia has been evacuated. I go back to my Quad. I refuse to be alone, so I ring the doorbell of my neighbor from the south of Brazil, that guy who takes pills and has a distant lover. He's not home either. From home, I call Gastão Abrantes. Nothing. Hildo. Nothing. Anyway, I don't know why I'm seeking out the company of those two; they wouldn't understand my problem. I just can't be alone. Heloisa. No. But isn't she one of my best friends? Anyway, I could change the story a little bit and put someone else in Renato's place. That's it. Heloisa isn't home either. Brasilia has certainly been evacuated.

I pick up a whiskey. It's six in the evening, still very early. I put on an Elis Regina record. I drink my second. I think about Luciano. I drink my third. I think about the two of us together. The bedroom. My fourth. I decide to call. No. My fifth: I fall asleep in the living room and awake at ten thirty. Shit! Now I'm not going to be able to sleep so early. All right. I'll read until dawn. Why would I be afraid of the night? Why would I be afraid of myself? The problem is the combination of the two: the night and I dialoguing, facing up to each other. No, I'll read a book, two books, and I will be okay.

But aren't I going to have dinner? I get to the kitchen but haven't the least desire to cook. The rice that the maid left in the oven is barely enough for a forkful. So I go out. Do I go to Feijão Verde or to that pizza place on W-3? No. Enough misery. Today, my anguish deserves the Tarantella. With this crappy salary of a University of Brasilia professor, I haven't been there for centuries. Today, I deserve it, today, this dirty Sunday.

I order a *carpaccio* as a starter. While I wait, I drink a whiskey and look at the sparse customers. Brasilia is so bureaucratic that on Sunday, at ten forty, the restaurants are already almost empty, just a couple on the upper level. The waiter almost didn't want to let me go up, but I insisted. I don't like to stay on the lower level, and besides, that pianist bothers me. When we are irritated, any music forced on us gets on our nerves. The couple upstairs: She is a bottle blonde, with sprayed-down hair and heavy makeup. She wears too much jewelry and sits up vainly in her seat. He must be in his fifties, big-bellied, gray-haired. A lawyer's ring shines on his finger. He is drinking whiskey. The bottle with a little ribbon is on the table. She's only drinking orange juice. She smokes noisily and lets her earrings swing like two golden balls as she talks. They talk loudly, and I am not interested in their conversation. How I would love to be Finnish right now and not understand crap of what Mr. Congressman and Mrs. Congressman are talking about.

My *carpaccio* arrives. I order a Chilean wine and a veal steak. The wine leads me by the hand. Luciano and I listen to music alone in the cold apartment. There is a lot of wind, and it is wet outside.

The dinner was magnificent. I hope I can forget the bill by tomorrow.

When I get home, my hands can do nothing else but obey the gesture suggested by the Chilean wine: I dial the number of my student Luciano. No. I hang up. What craziness! Have I thought of the embarrassment of being told off by one of my students? I could never look at him again in class. In the meantime, who says I am calling for any other reason than simply to talk, to have a chat on a Sunday night?

"Hello, Julio? Everything cool?"
"Great, and you?"
"The same. But what a surprise! What's your pleasure?"
I couldn't resist. I was beside myself.
"Nothing. That is...Sunday night...I thought of calling you....
"Julio...."
The boy takes my protection away. He treats me with the intimacy of a neighbor or of someone who has always known my feelings. He is certainly insightful enough to have perceived my wounded looks of jealousy that night at Renato's house. Instead of feeling embarrassed, I should have invented some pretext, a concert, a play, a party.... We should never go in unarmed like that, as if shooting in the dark, without a parachute.

Luciano—useless and dangerous dreams, maybe the consequence of tedium.

I go back to the sofa. The headlights of the cars slide over the surface of the blinds, which beat lightly against the wall. The breeze is beginning to bring the long-off smell of rain.

I pick up the telephone and dial Luciano's number. I *need* to talk to him. The telephone keeps on ringing. What luck if he isn't home!

"Hello?"
"Luciano? It's Julio."
I avoid identifying myself as a professor.
"Julio? Hi!" he greets me enthusiastically.
"How are you doing?"
"Me? I feel like I miss you. I'm calling because I miss you."
"You miss me?"
"Yes, I miss you."

A frightening silence comes from the other end.

"Julio…"

Sometimes Luciano stutters.

"Am I invading your space? But I was just calling you…"

"Look, pardon me, but I had a rehearsal early today, and I'm really sleepy. Please excuse me but…"

"I just need to tell you one thing."

A new silence, an impatient silence, fortifies like a wall but offers a gap.

"I don't feel any attraction for you. That is, physical, physical attraction, understand?"

Luciano tries to interrupt me.

"What I feel is great affection, a great affection that I cannot explain, and I don't even know why I called you at this time of the night. It's just to tell you that I don't feel anything, nothing, just a tremendous affection…I miss you…sometimes."

Some three seconds drag by in abysmal silence.

"Have you been with anyone lately?"

I'm not expecting that question. I'm completely taken aback.

"Just some sporadic flings."

"Some sporadic flings?" he echoes.

"Yes, in fact, the other day, I was telling Mauricio that you seem rather sad."

"Me? You think so?"

"Look, we need to talk."

He finally pulls out his verdict. "You think so? Yes, I think that we need to talk."

"I would like to. I really wanted to…I don't know. We could have lunch together tomorrow, Monday. But not at the cafeteria, of course, some other place in the city…. I really wanted to talk with you."

As he speaks, my heart starts beating faster. "I know of a new vegetarian restaurant in the North Wing. We could talk there."

I hate vegetarian restaurants, but of course I accept.

After we say good-bye, I feel a horrible sensation burning me inside. I have definitely crossed a line that I have never before contemplated. And even if Luciano had wanted to seem friendlier toward the end of the call, my guilt leaves me feeling inevitably beaten.

I drink another whiskey. Then another one. It's useless to try to sleep. I had slept from six to ten thirty. It is too late to call anyone. So then I'll just wait, sitting in the living room, listening to the same record, the record player in repeat mode. I think that after all, he has treated me well, and has even agreed to have lunch with me the next day. I get to the point where everything is spinning around, my own voice coming out in a higher register, mellifluous, and I fall asleep on the sofa.

I didn't turn the record player off until morning.

6

It's not a matter now of hanging on to her, like Proust's prisoner, which would only be torturous for both of us, but rather gaining her confidence. The time is perfect for us to close ourselves up at home while I paint and Heloisa reads. Now, I only paint for her. When I make a stroke, I choose a color, an object, or a composition of some sort and dedicate my emotions and my thoughts to her. The way she devours books, she seems like a moth. Sometimes I stupidly think that she reads only to isolate herself, to keep away from me. Maybe that's why, out of stupid jealousy, I've lent her the book from my nightstand: an anthology of poems by Cecília Meireles.

Heloisa interrupted me and looked briefly at my work in progress. Then she went to the kitchen, certainly to make lunch. Renato usually calls on the flimsiest of pretexts. Just yesterday, he called to say that Heloisa had forgotten a coat at home, and he offered to bring it by.

"I don't want to see that guy," I said in a low voice and with gestures.

Heloisa answered that he could keep the coat, but he insisted on returning it.

Downer. Absolute downer. It's not that I think that Heloisa is going to go back to the son of a bitch after all that's happened, luckily for me. (Actually, I don't have much reason to call him son of a bitch, in spite of all the shit he has put Heloisa through. After all, I never showed much discretion in coming on to her.) No, Heloisa is not crazy enough to go back to Renato. It's not possible. After all that I have been able to do, it would exasperate me to live without her at my side even though she sometimes retreats into herself. What craziness! In these quiet hours, I think about how everything happened in such an incredible way. Deep inside, I never believed that one day she would come to live with me and share such a deep friendship. I know that she loved Renato a lot; I know that she still loves him, but her pain is too deep for her to be able to reestablish her relationship with him, to put back the pieces of an impossible life together.

I was never suspicious of Renato's tendencies, to tell the truth. Nor did I wonder about his little escapades into the *demimonde* of Brasilia. What a deal, huh? Julio is a tomb. Never, even in an instant of anger, did he let escape any allusion to his friend's secret life. A queer who'd have guessed it? "One more" loose on the plain.... Could it be that now, as the new director, he is going to continue doing his little things? Or is he going to get married again? Could well be. I just don't want him to get the idea that Heloisa is the perfect woman for him. One night, at his mother's house on the lake—one of their temporary separations when he fled back to Leonor's lap—after a few whiskeys, Renato confessed to me his idea of Heloisa: she was the perfect wife; she came from a traditional family in Rio; she had been educated in a respectable Catholic girls' school; she spoke French and English; she knew how to entertain and could converse on a variety of topics; she was cultured, et cetera, et cetera. The only quality he failed to praise was her sexual performance, a quality that probably was of little interest to him, we might say in passing. I know about Renato's past. According to some girlfriends of mine who knew him in Rio, he had a long affair with one girl/young lady, and then a short one with Heloisa. What a coincidence! The two girls were socially connected, and Heloisa—although not wealthy—had a good name. I assume, therefore, that he may hook up with *a parvenu* like that to serve as a decoration for his rise through the ministry, one stupid enough not to discover his inevitable escapades. If so many people do that, why not Renato, too? A façade, that's all those people think about.

Sometimes I watch Dad: he has changed so much...he was so different years ago.... Once, we had a talk in the country house about that. It was after lunch; I had had a few strong drinks, and then everything came out. I said that he was a great disappointment to me. The words were strong, but they came out. I couldn't do anything about it, and his face withered up. It really did. You know, when a face shrinks up like the quick wilting of a flower? I got scared; I didn't know what was coming. After it withered, his face turned red, and he got furious. But it was true: I remember what he was like in the old days when I was small. I even mentioned it to my brothers the other day in Rio, and to Heloisa. Dad liked to read and listen to classical music, cooped up in his library. But if we came in, he would greet us with the greatest affection. He'd put us on his lap, play games, tell stories, tell us about what he was reading, what he was listening to. He gave us coconut or caramel candies that he always kept in a lacquer box. Later, when I was a teenager, he would have political discussions with me. He told me about the operations of government, the three branches, Montesquieu, Rousseau, Voltaire, Tocqueville, Diderot, the French Revolution, Greek democracy, modern democracy, et cetera. Sitting on his lap in the library, I would listen to him with much greater attention than I would give my teachers in school, and his voice would fill the room and rise up among the shelves and the books, "all of them read by my father," and I believed him. He was a congressman at that time.

Years later, we came to live in Brasilia. I didn't understand anything. Suddenly, I had to leave my friends behind to come to this dead city. But it's the nation's capital, mother said to console me. As a teenager, I adapted quickly, but Dad changed. He became distant, preoccupied with his social life, his pedantic and arrogant friends. I almost didn't see him anymore, and mother seemed to be bored with the political life of the "capital," which for us was merely a village, and he would often go to Rio. My brothers moved there as soon as they graduated. I wanted to leave, because I wanted to study art in Europe. He sent me to Paris, where I lived for four years. I came back without a diploma, and he was furious. Really, I don't have anything to do with academies; my painting has to be free. When a professor would have me draw from a live model or a still life, I would lose interest, just because I had been told what to do. In classes on the history or philosophy of art, when a professor would impose his opinion on something, I couldn't keep quiet and would end up in an ugly argument. European professors don't let you argue with them, and with my temperament.... That's why I wasn't able to finish college. Fuck it! When I got back, I had to take care of my life, and I asked Dad for a job, since by that time, he was a senator. He answered that he could only get me work in Brasilia. It's a sort of punishment, but this part-time job gives me time to paint. Anyway, thanks to the emotional tranquility that Heloisa gives me, I can prepare carefully for my exhibit. If she leaves me suddenly, I don't know...I'll lose my bearings, and I think that I won't get another exhibit any time soon.

7

I went to visit Heloisa, and it was awful. When I rang the bell, I thought no one was going to answer. Maybe they looked through the peephole and hesitated to open, since I heard murmurings coming from inside. My state of concern actually stretched out the time: I probably didn't wait more than two or three minutes. Heloisa opened the door. She asked what I wanted. Now, what *would* I want? What could I want of her other than to make an apology? But I didn't. When I heard that question, I got a knot in my throat, and it took me a few seconds before I could say anything. I asked for my records, which she had brought with her. We began to have an argument right in the hallway of the building where Carla lives. A gray corridor covered in little tiles. There is a red fire extinguisher visible in the back. And Heloisa was shouting at me, tears running down her face behind her glasses. All that bothered me so much that I could hardly hear what she was yelling about. Suddenly, she turned around to get inside and came back with her hands full of records that she threw on top of me, toward the walls, and onto the floor. After that, she came at me, hitting and scratching. I grabbed her wrists, and then Carla appeared and grabbed her by the shoulders, squeezed her arms, and calmed her down. I had never seen Heloisa in that condition. She was always so contained…but I was shocked by the scene of my ex-wife being held up by Carla, crying. I left down the hallway disoriented and with the same knot in my throat.

At night, I went to have dinner with Elaine at the Gaf restaurant. She is a lovely girl. She's rich; her father was one of the pioneering businessmen in Brasilia. She lives on the lake, of course. Not only is she pretty, she is also fairly well informed. So we got along well. She has a velvety look and a voice hoarse from smoking cigarettes. She doesn't drink alcohol. She drank Coca-Cola the whole evening. Since that was not quite the case for me, I told her everything that had happened in the afternoon. Studying psychology at the CEUB, Elaine voiced her opinion that Heloisa is hysterical with a strong lesbian tendency. Of course, I had attenuated the colors a bit in telling what had brought about our breakup. Of course.

"But do you still love her?" Elaine asked me between drags on her cigarette.

"I don't know."

My answer disappointed her, I know. I turned my eyes to the pianist, the waiters, and those people in the Gaf, all atrociously out of style. Elaine seemed upset. I left her off at her house, and, when I got home, served myself a nightcap. The telephone rang. It was Julio, half drunk. He told me that after a long talk the night before by telephone, Luciano had left him waiting for hours at a restaurant. Poor Julio, always colliding and smashing up in bad relationships. He dreams too much. He starts wanting someone and pursues that dream until he becomes consumed in delirium and alcohol, like all those insects that allow themselves to be burned up by a lamp. He talked, talked, and talked. I just listened. He accused me of seducing and having sex with the boy. "Look, dude, if he wanted to fuck me," I interrupted him, "you have nothing to do with it. Shit!" He hung up. Yes, I think I was rather gross with him...but the guy begins to offend me suddenly— me, who was listening to him attentively at that time of night! And what if I had been sleeping? I had thought of calling him back, but no, I fell asleep after a few gulps.

8

The red fire extinguisher in the back of the gray hallway and he in front were exposed to my fury, a fury that inundated me, leaving me completely blind—and he made me throw all the records in his face. I scratched him and hit him until I just wanted to see his face a bloody paste, like the red fire extinguisher on the gray wall. But Carla took hold of me and wouldn't let me wound him the way he still wounds me. Oh, when I saw Renato in the hallway trying to play the good guy and under the ridiculous pretext of claiming possession of *my* records! He comes here to Carla's house not to see me, but for the simple purpose of reigniting in me all that emotion from the horrible scene in his office. And to think that he always cheated on me, not with women, not with my friends, as what often happens, but with little boys, with fags that he picked up at the bus station. Julio knew everything but never said a word to me. That's why I only trust Carla and nobody else in the world. But I don't feel anything for her beyond a great friendship. No, I do not feel any desire for her or for any other woman. When she comes to lie down on the sofa in the living room where I sleep, I can't help but say gently, "Not today, Carla." And I know that she has understood, because I have repeated this phrase for months on end without our having any physical intimacy. In turn, Carla doesn't demand anything; she doesn't complain, which makes me like her even more.

Yesterday, however, she came in drunk after a little party at work and grabbed me by force. I tried to get away, but she was able to kiss me. I don't like that, and only now, I'm beginning to think about whether I should stay here. I've been talking to Mom on the telephone, and she insists that I move in with her in Rio. However, the weird situation of having to share a house with that Bob doesn't encourage me even a little, especially lately when he has been burning through

Mom's money without any scruples at all. That I won't tolerate: watching with my arms crossed as the little pimp exploits my mother. It seems that they already have a joint bank account. And a credit card. No, look, I prefer to stay far away from all that, and if sometimes I inevitably get wind of something, I think that's still better than being there. I would fight with that boy every day. I can't live with Father either. He and Marluce lead their own lives on the ranch in Itaipava, and I don't have the tiniest intention of settling in the country.

So where do I go? At thirty-five years of age, without family, I have only Carla's friendship. I don't seek out Julio anymore after I found out about all the crap. Well, he wasn't in a position where he could talk to me, but…at least he could have made me see something, instead of letting me sit around like an idiot. Oh, to be deceived is the worst thing in the world! And to know that even if I trusted Renato implicitly and thought of him as an intellectual preoccupied with his career, while I worked at the university or at home, he was chasing after little boys. That's why he left me alone so much. I didn't understand; I thought that he was just worried and that he was taking rides in the car to calm down. And Julio knew everything. They went out together. These are the memories—memories of each scene I lived through, my being deceived, his deceiving me—that hurt the most, that irritates me the most.

Really, what I wanted to do was to contrive some great revenge. Revenge, yes, instead of hiding like a hunted animal. That's when the great madness happened.

One weekday, I ran into Inacio at the club. The rains had called a truce, and the waters of the pool were so quiet that an insect would make the surface ripple visibly. There were a few clouds in the sky. In the club, only waiters talked, bored and far off the sound of a ball hitting the tennis court: ping, ping, ping. I sat in front of the pool, opened a book, and ordered an orange juice from the waiter. The noise of the ball came to a stop. The wind made the leaves rattle, blowing the driest ones to the ground. Ever since I was a little girl, I have had the impression that if the wind blows softly, it brings a warning: something is about to happen. I heard footsteps but didn't raise my eyes from the book. I'm reading the poems of Cecília Meireles that

Carla lent to me. The steps came closer. I looked to the right, and Inacio came walking in my direction with the tennis racket over his shoulder. He was more deeply tanned. He walked with that characteristic step of his with his legs slightly bowed. He greeted me and sat down. He ordered lemonade. The wind continued to blow in the trees; the water in the pool puckered up. There was a threatening softness in the air. Almost in silence, we looked at each other. A dark bird from the fields cut across the yard and went to the lake, emitting a strident sound. "The grass gets so green after the rains...." I comment. He didn't answer; he just hit the racket lightly against the edge of the table. I got restless when conversation fell into these gaps of silence. Then I looked for something to talk about, as if it were really necessary to say something, or as if words could build a bridge between two cases of loneliness.

"Gastão thinks that the pavilion over there reminds him of the pavilion in the *Maias*." I took that sentence from out of my pocket for no particular reason, looking at the garden and the lake. Ever literary, Inacio limited himself to a smile without looking at me. Of course, he had never read *Os Maias*.[68]

"Gastão is something else," he said after a few seconds. "What book is that you're reading?"

"Cecília Meireles."

I became quiet as I realized the meaning of the question. "What does that have to do with anything?" Inacio put the racket down on the table and moved his jaw, as if chewing something. Then he looked at me. The wind stopped, the bird shrieked. There was a sort of immobilization of time and an abolition of space: I didn't have my feet on the ground of the club anymore, but I was suspended in a vacuum. Inacio's glare cut through me like a blade.

Suddenly, a sign of rain: a smell of wetness and gray clouds blowing over from the other side of the lake. Strange, in absolute silence, we got up and went to his house. When we got to his apartment, the rain broke loose. He didn't offer me anything; he didn't

---

[68] *Os Maias (The Maias)* 1888: this long and involved novel is one of the most important of Eça de Queiroz,. It recounts the saga of the Maia family in Lisbon as a social satire.

put any music on. He pulled off my glasses, hugged me, kissed me, and took off my clothes.

Now I know what is happening to me. It's what I always wanted. I can't live at Carla's house anymore. I need to get up the courage to talk with Renato. I am finally going to accept his constant proposals that I come back, but he is going to have to accept my terms.

9

I waited for hours at the vegetarian restaurant. The dark-skinned waitress with curly hair was already smiling at me in a funny way, as if she could guess the reason for my useless wait. There is always a sort of sadness about this kind of restaurant. I think the customers become depressed and yellowed from their excess health. Everyone's skin has a bilious-looking color. Nevertheless, Luciano likes this kind of restaurant. He gets all excited about vegetarian or "organic" food. But he didn't come. He didn't come as he promised. I've already drunk rivers of orange juice with carrot and strawberry juice. Hunger came so I decided to order. I chewed that rice and those insipid vegetables and greens and tried to give them some flavor by soaking them in soy sauce. And no Luciano. It felt like a pie was spread across my face—a big, creamy pie, just as flavorless as the rest of the food in this place. The cream slid to my mouth, and the filling hit my whole face, covering my eyes. Little by little, that feeling of being ground up inside returned, as if an instrument of torture had been inserted in my body. My hunger passed. I crossed my knife and fork without finishing the meal and looked at the waitress who eyed me with pity. Luciano. So why did he promise to come? You yourself suggested the encounter and the conversation, and now this immense pie in my face. I looked at the saloon-type door for the millionth time. Unknown people continued to enter, moving the two flaps in an infinite coming and going. I paid the bill and got up, always with my eyes fixed on the saloon door through which no Luciano passed.

Stood up with pie in my face. Everyone carries a bunch of different pies around in life, but now I have the clear sensation that this scene has happened to me many times in exactly the same way: me seated in a vegetarian restaurant waiting for someone who never comes. Gastão Abrantes would say smiling that it is an eternal payback. Except I hope never to relive this situation: it's like entering a movie theater by mistake and watching a really bad film for the second time.

10

I tried not to drink at the party. It was hard. The hours pass deplorably slowly. People seem unable to escape the banality of their daily lives. Topics get more and more moldy. Gestures and attitudes go by degrees from a state of relative control to one of intolerable vulgarity. We also run the risk of crowning ourselves with such vulgarity when we go overboard in the number of aperitifs we drink. Nonetheless, on these occasions, we show a high degree of tolerance for the inebriate, even those who are most predictable, the prototypes, those who have their self-regulation meters a bit out of whack even when sober, but who destroy it completely when they supply a little too much "fuel" to their bodies. Because sometimes we drink, sometimes we drown. Then Dionysus embraces us and does whatever he wants with us. It is these calculation mistakes about the number of shots imbibed, this chemical deception measured in fluid ounces, that Heloisa does not forgive in me.

Anyway, there's no greater supplication. Look, they throw us into an arena—or rather a garden—an oasis with gurgling fountains and throbbing palm trees, and languid, Oriental music, and they invite us to drink from the spouts. You like it; the liquid carries the flavor of dry, acidic fruits, dates, figs, grapes, and raisins, and you try one more swallow. The water is enchanted. It comes from the abyss, from the center of the earth, from a river that starts in paradise and returns there. It lightens, bringing happiness to the fatigued breast of the traveler. It invades the viscera, and you want more. And more. Until someone pulls you by the arm: "No! Be careful!" you insist, leaning over the marble side of the fountain, and there you loll about, delighting in the secrets of the sacred waters. But once again, they tie your arms; the water is cut off. You extend your tongue, anxious for a few more droplets in order to share the company of the gods, but it is shut off to you. Then you again become the child that has awakened in you: you scream, cry, and kick your feet; you want the water from the subterranean river that washed the sadness from your deserts.

This is what I kept myself from doing to please Heloisa: I tied myself to the highest mast of the ship, or I put wax in my ears in order not to hear the singing from the fountains. The party dragged on, but this time we didn't argue, not even when we got home or on the following day. Even better, my controlled behavior served as an unintended strategy. On Sunday morning, while she read the newspapers, I decided to take coffee in to her. Distracted, she took the cup and dropped in the sugar without taking her eyes off the article she was reading. I approached her shoulder slowly and gave her a kiss on the face. As I realized that unlike in similar situations in the past, she didn't react, saying, "Not now, Carla," I moistened her neck and ear with my lips. I gave her caresses. Finally, I took her in my arms. When her body was all mine, like a meadow stretching under moonlight, I savored the greatest conquest. But before raising my red flag of victory, I feared to lose it immediately—as badly engendered battles are lost, as poorly guarded treasures are lost. It is necessary to reinforce the watchmen in the towers and on the castle walls, and not allow oneself to be taken over by the imminent foreign invasion.

11

Madame Leonor, in spite of having thought that the decision for Heloisa and me to separate was right, is of the opinion that I should wait a while before "creating another union." To tell the truth, she never liked Heloisa. She said that she was a girl with ulterior motives, that she came from who-knows-where, and that she would only be concerned with taking on our name and position. As if we still had anything. Mother still lives in the times when Father was an ambassador, the time of the false glitter—which ended up rusting, without her realizing it. After she was widowed, Leonor still considered herself an ambassadress at her peak, and she tried to maintain her old friendships. But when she realized that she was being put aside, when she was not invited to this or that reception, she became furious, and her migraines returned and left her for days cloistered in her room. She only comes out with dark glasses on, since, as she says, "This sun of Brasilia is like a knife," and her headaches increase. One Sunday, I invited Elaine and another couple over to swim in the pool. Mother suddenly appeared, always wearing her dark glasses, and when she saw me opening a can of beer, she began to shout, as if I were still a boy, calling me an alcoholic who began to drink early in the morning (when it was already afternoon), saying that I brushed my teeth with whiskey and other such absurdities. It was the first time that Elaine had seen her, and I don't need to say what sort of an impression she made. She was horrified, scared of Madame Leonor, who came toward me for no reason at all, like a bird of prey.

"I think it's best for us to leave," I heard Fabinho whisper to his wife.

I simply turned my back to her and left with my friends. In the car, Fabinho decided to open his can of beer, which, until then, he had left "virgin," having immobilized his finger in the flip top when he witnessed that inexplicable fury from Leonor. The beer exploded right there, like champagne, soaking the roof of the car and dripping like rain, maybe commemorating our freedom.

I returned home late, walking in sheepishly, as if I were wearing those fluffy slippers from the museum in Petrópolis, quiet, sneaking down the hall to avoid waking Mother—like a teenager. From my room, I called Heloisa. They weren't home. The phone rang so much it seemed like it was broken. In bed, I thought about whether I would marry again. Elaine is pretty, she has shining eyes, a certain charm but…the other day, a Saturday, she had a party at her house north of the lake. Fine. Her parents are nice. Her father, kind of fat, told me about the early days of the city, when everything was red clay. He was half drunk and repeated his story to me several times.

"This here was a campground…It was nothing like what you see here now. How this place has grown!"

The mother, rather retiring, limited herself to greeting me, but she would come up to me all the time to see if I needed anything. Elaine has brothers: one is a sportsman, black belt in karate, and the other is crazy about motorcycles and race cars. When they greeted me, I felt their callused hands. The house has some things that I don't like: a neo-Greco-Roman style, a fountain with colored lights at the entrance, and statues of dwarves in the garden. Anyway, you can see that the pioneer prospered: the house is large and comfortable, in spite of the pictures in the living room that are not exactly to my taste.

12

The doctor confirmed it: I am pregnant. This afternoon, all alone, I contemplate the ground after the rain, and I feel fertile, full of life, ready to confer upon the world a duplication of myself, regenerating, like all females around the world in the heart of nature.

But what is to become of him? The child of a casual connection, product of an irresponsible desire—I must admit—of an attraction without further consequences? I hesitate about whether to tell Carla. I hesitate about whether to tell Renato. "If you want to abort..." the doctor sounded me out. I just shook my head no; I thought of squeezing my belly as a sign of protection, but I simply got up and looked at a vacant lot full of garbage next to the clinic. On the way home, I speculated about the future that I had just given myself: a child alters all my perspectives. Deep inside, I still don't know what I wanted to prove by my decision to keep it. I've never had an abortion; I've never before been pregnant. I got to the point of thinking that Renato was sterile, and perhaps he is, although he has never told me anything. Renato never expressed the slightest desire to have a child. If I brought the subject up, he would dissemble; he said that children make noise, they get sick, they are expensive, and after they grow up, they don't want to have anything to do with their parents. But I always wanted to have maybe just one child. "All women..." my mother would say if she heard me now. So-and-so has two—a boy and a girl, and when she writes to me or calls me with stories about her children, I have to admit my envy.

"And you guys?" she asked me.

"We are thinking about giving it some time...you know, it's still pretty soon...we aren't even thinking about it yet...." That's what I usually tell my friends, who would be surprised at my revealing redness if they weren't at the other end of the line.

Renato required me to put in my diaphragm regularly.

"We could try, at least once."

"No and no. It's too soon to have children."

Now, this embryo is taking shape inside of me. I don't feel any sign yet. Only when my womb starts to grow and I feel the first movements, would I'll be sure. How crazy I am. And this child? Is it going to look like Inacio, like me, a mixture of the two of us? Those questions and all the ones that inevitably come up about the sex and the name to be chosen come to me over and over the whole afternoon. I made the decision, then, not to give it either the father's or the mother's name: I don't want it to be a repetition of either of us, but rather a different creature full of energy, pulsating with the rhythm of life.

If Renato doesn't accept him, I'll have him anyway. I'll raise him even if I have to do it alone. I'll move to another city, to Belo Horizonte, to the south. I don't know. What I do know is that a dream has come true. Or is coming true. And I have to take my task all the way to the end.

13

The half-naked drag queen rolls around at the top of the metal-bar tower where the loudspeakers were installed. There, among pennants and flags, is where the big canvas awning is attached, covering the bar-buffet. "She" dances, dressed only in a tiny bikini bottom, her body covered in purple stars. She waves and throws kisses to the people. "It looks like she's the owner of the party," so said Mauricio, who had invited me. The bad thing was that the friend of his had come along, the pianist from the bar. An ugly dude. I heard that the two of them had had an affair. In this way, Mauricio disappoints me. More specifically, now that we are talking frankly, it was Aldo who told me:

"That boy is a little slut. He screws anyone. All you have to do is phone him and say, 'Shall we go out?' and he accepts, and then puts out. Try him. His number is 273...."

I didn't call—that afternoon—but on another day, I did, and he asked me if I didn't want to go to a great party north of the lake, at the home of a certain Orlando, a queer famous around Brasilia. Mauricio didn't say those words exactly, but the adjective *famous* not only fits with the noun *queer*, but it is also appropriate because of the wild social events that he organized. So there was Orlando, presiding magnificently over the dance, flying around the yard surrounding the house.

People were dancing on the veranda and in the house.

Suddenly, a great tiredness came over me, a weariness, a sensation of *déjà vu* so great that I felt like leaving, and I shared my feeling with Mauricio, who answered:

"Oh, stay a little longer...We just got here."

Meanwhile, the impression of being worn out, the idea of promoting a "crazy" party with all stops pulled, with all possible freedom, as if it were a new idea of incomparable daring, as if a generation before ours had not done it a thousand times, as if we ourselves had not gone through this before, made me sick to my stomach. Not for moral stature—I'm far from that—but that queen showing off up there over the colored circus tent filled me with tedium, and not even Mauricio's presence convinced me to stay. I said good-bye to him, in spite of his dry, ill-humored answer; I said good-bye even though I took the risk that he might sleep with the pianist again that night.

14

I can't say anything: the apartment is filled with a resounding emptiness. She went away. I can't stay here. Everything reminds me of her. Every corner, every book, every song. And the smell? Is it her smell that rises from the sofa, from the sheets?

Tomorrow, I'm going to Rio to spend a month. From there, I'll ask Father to sell or rent the apartment. Let him do whatever he wants with all of this. I can't see this living room again, the furniture, that bedroom. I'll stay with my brother at his place, and that's it.

How can this be? A tornado and then suddenly an emptiness. Hollow. Heloisa revealed her decision to me when we got back from Julio's book signing. She didn't want to go, but I insisted. After all, Julio was always her great friend. Of course, Heloisa, he wasn't going to make trouble and put you against your husband. He didn't want to tell you that your husband liked men.

Julio was happy. Finally, his book of short stories got published.

My exhibit, then, goes to hell. I'm going to send the paintings and my materials to Rio as unaccompanied baggage. And I'll look for a job and an apartment there. My brother says he can find me part-time work at his office, but I'm really thinking about giving drawing and painting classes to children. That has always been my dream.

Live here? I can't do it anymore.

When she told me she was going, my legs started to shake. The ground fell out from under me. My vision clouded up. I gagged. I sweated, and I couldn't even outline any resistance or think of some way to convince her to change her mind and stay. Horrible. And her coldness! When we came in from the book signing, Heloisa sat on the sofa and told me everything. I couldn't believe what I was hearing. She was simply crazy! To go back to Renato after all that! No, I couldn't believe it, and I just kept quiet, with a knot in my throat.

When the door banged shut, I was scared. Scared of the house. I got in my car and went out. It took a while before I could cry, maybe for fear of what could happen next. After so much effort, after managing to have her here with me, everything falls apart, and she goes right back to Renato, and I can't understand anything. Everything in life comes to an end. Even life itself. I will pack my bags and leave tomorrow.

15

I open the door, and she comes in slowly. I hold her arms delicately, kiss her face, and lightly touch her abdomen. We go sit on the sofa. I shelter her in my arms. Heloisa. Everything has passed. It was a delirium and a tempest. It's over. Now you're going to have the child you always wanted. I don't know if I can have sex with a pregnant woman. But I will. I'll do everything for you now, Heloisa. I swear that I am going to behave. I'll be good to you. To you and your child. Our child.

"Turn on the TV?" she asks.

I obey. I loosen my tie, unbutton my shirt, take off my shoes, and stretch my legs out onto the coffee table. She slides down to the carpet, lies over my legs, and caresses my feet. The television is showing a soccer match. She gets up and sits in the easy chair, her back to the TV. She seems to be distant.

"Do you want to see something else?"

She shakes her head no. I pick up my legs from off the table (Madame Leonor always scolded me for that), put my shoes halfway on, and let myself stare at the game like an idiot.

16

I hesitate before ringing the bell. It's strange, but it doesn't feel like I'm at the front door of my own house. I feel a terror and attraction for him. I don't know if I'll ring. I squeeze my sweaty fingers together and look at my luggage: an unclosed suitcase that belonged to Mother and a carrying bag. Nothing else to do: I ring the bell. He takes a long time to answer. Maybe he isn't home.

Renato finally opens the door. He has a relaxed air about him, his hair poorly combed, his shirt wrinkled, coming halfway out of his brown pants—that pair that I detest, but he probably doesn't remember my criticism of him. The smell. Yes, it's the lavender he usually wears. Deep inside, I hope he'll say, "Come in," but he doesn't. I cross the threshold, and his perfume gets stronger and stronger. I look at his bottle-green eyes, which reveal his distrust. It looks as if he doesn't believe my decision. He holds my arms firmly, almost hurting me; he kisses me on the left cheek and puts his palm on my stomach in a gesture that acknowledges my state. Well, I myself told him. We sit on the sofa; he hugs me. I don't want to exchange a word, so I ask him to turn the TV on. Okay. They are showing a soccer match, a game I hate. The monotonous movements of legs and the ball from one side of the field to the other, struggling to reach the net on the right side or the net on the left side. And always with the monotone voice of the announcer who describes and comments on what we are seeing.

I don't know what to do. I don't want to justify anything, and I'm feeling regret over what I have done. There's this desire to flee from here, but where would I go? Renato is my safe port. I feel the warmth of his body, that same restless body that moves away from me to go about the darkness and the overpasses of this dead city. I then feel tenderness for that body at my side. I sit on the floor. I lie on his knees and caress his feet. He doesn't show the slightest reaction. He was always like that with me. The game tires me out. I can barely see the television, and I remain like that, immobile, without reaction, since nothing can exist except in this way.

17

Doors that open, doors that close under the strong afternoon light: this is Brasilia. An empty apartment, the breeze making the blinds beat against the wall, the lake taking on a shade loaded with blue as the sun reddens the horizon. This is Brasilia, and I'm leaving. From one moment to the next, my life changes: I accept the invitation to work at a college in São Paulo, my book of short stories finally getting published, a three-year wait. That's how it is in Brazil: it takes so long to publish a book that when it comes out, it seems obsolete. Finally, my friends went to the launching at the Book House. It was rewarding, in spite of my dislike of this type of celebration. Even Luciano came— who would have thought? I wrote a dry dedication for him. If I had been sincere, I would have broken up in declarations of love for him, in Alexandrines, or I would have written the worst insults because of what happened at the vegetarian restaurant, depending on my level of alcohol at that time of night. When the party was over, we left together, Heloisa, Carla, and I. We went to the Beirut. Heloisa had drunk a little more than her usual and confessed her indignation to me for never having told her about her ex-husband. Shit, how could I do something like that? I wasn't going to go up to her and say, "Look here, my friend, did you know that your husband is gay?" I wouldn't. I think that now she understood, but what left me completely awestruck was her revealing to me, just when Carla went to the bathroom, that she intended to return to Renato.

"Are you nuts?" I said.

But she seemed very sure of herself. She gave explanations, just as everyone finds one when they want something. They sounded logical, as they usually do at first. Later, I came to the conclusion that she is utterly crazy to go back to a guy who did what he did. Crazy. Her eyes were shiny with drink.

"You do whatever you think is best," I finished off.

My move was yesterday. Mauricio came here, because he said he was interested in buying the living room curtains, as well as some pictures that I didn't want anymore. His father, a military man, bought my VW bug for the family. I opened some beers, we talked, and, suddenly, in the hallway, after hanging up the telephone from a call from work, the boy planted a tremendous kiss on my mouth. I was astonished. I never thought. He is rather good-looking. I hugged him, and we ended up screwing right there in the empty apartment. It was night already. I did him against the wall of my room, then he masturbated me, and we fell on the rough carpet. Today, my knees are scraped. But that doesn't matter. Gastão, with whom I have entrusted my deepest secrets, had invited me to sleep at his house, and then asked when he saw me:

"What was it like?"

"Good."

I like Mauricio. I want to believe that I like him, but I'm afraid—a deep fear of beginning the whole wheel of torture over again. At least Mauricio is real, palpable, and not like Flaubert's golden idol whose fingers are not to be touched, like Luciano. Besides the fear, now I don't think that either of us believes this relationship would work. I'm leaving; he's staying. He has to finish his studies; I have to try for better luck in the miserable profession of being a professor in São Paulo. Meanwhile, I write to let out my anguish and my need for fantasy. A friend of mine kept a long-distance relationship going for years. Who knows about Mauricio and me? No. No. Everything evaporates on our way to the airport, I know. He knows, too. But it was good. It happened, and I needed it to happen. It happened just as all good things happen: unexpectedly. And unexpectedly he may reappear in my life. Or there would be another Mauricio on another night, in another empty apartment, on the eve of departure.

This afternoon, Mauricio came back to pick up his curtains and his pictures. We agreed to meet in São Paulo. I'll send him my new address as soon as I have it. We said good-bye affectionately in the empty apartment, but he insisted on taking me to the airport. I have to say good-bye to Heloisa and Renato. Carla called me up drunk, saying that she was leaving, too.

I go to their Quad. My plane leaves at nine, and it's already seven o'clock. Now, it's Mauricio who's giving me a ride. Funny. I say to him:

"Wait for me here, okay?"

I get in the elevator. Doors that open, doors that close. I ring the bell with some trepidation. No one answers.

Suddenly, I realize that the door is not locked. Lightly and silently, I open it and see a strange sight: Renato sitting on the sofa, his shirt messed up, his tie loose, his feet halfway out of his shoes, his glassy eyes watching a soccer game on television. Heloisa is sitting beside him, immobile, her luggage still in the middle of the living room. They seemed not to notice my presence, and they had their hands interlocked. I thought of saying that I had come to say good-bye, but I don't know why I held back. I wanted to get out of there, and that's just what I did. I left in silence and turned my back on them. I didn't tell Mauricio what I had seen. We went on the airport, since I was already late.

It seems that I'm looking at the Axis for the last time. This passage looks as if the designs from our geometry notebooks have landed here, and then come alive, illustrating and proving their schematic existence. Does this long highway go right there, to infinity, an infinity of red earth touched by the evening? No, it no longer exists. There two parallel lines meet. My father, a mathematics teacher, would say:

"This is very philosophical! No one has been there…but meet they do." I can see from here how these two lines that mark the edges of the road touch at the horizon. But they are parallel, not convergent, and therefore do not really touch, since the point on the horizon is just an optical illusion. Isn't the concept of infinity really just an abstraction? The universe may be infinite. And beyond the universe? What could there be beyond the continuous explosion? Hollowness, emptiness, nothing, God? So there, the two parallel lines touch each other, according to my father. The vanishing point. This is what we are trying to reach: a point that can never be reached. And why do we always travel in that direction, crazily, like the desire of the moth for the farthest star—as in Shelley's poem—headed not to the airport, but to the vanishing point, which is simply an illusion? A mere optical illusion. But whatever it is, we are headed there. If I look back, I see some pieces of the road through the twilight. I again see snapshots from childhood: a straw hat carried away by the wind, a yard with mango and guava trees, the black face of my nanny—images that fall to dust in the half light. But before me, I have only this darkness and two lines that converge at a point, my goal. Why, for what, I don't know. I simply go on. Toward a point that is a pure mirage.